celtic
stars

DELANEY
RHODES

Moonlite Publishing

ISBN-10: * 0985332646
ISBN-13: * 9780985332648

Cover Design by Kim Killion
Layout by Penoaks Publishing, http://penoaks.com

What Readers Are Saying
About *The Celtic Steel Series*

"Great read couldn't put it down. Can't wait for the next book in the series. You rank up there with Diana Gabaldon of the Highlander series."

B. Breen

"I love the story – I thought it was the right mix of romance, a strong female character, historical setting, and magic/paranormal..."

A. Alayna

"What a FUN new author with a fabulous and well written storyline! I wasn't sure what to expect, but found myself so pulled into the story that I HAD to finish it before I could move onto my daily "to-do's"; needless to say I recommend doing any and all chores before starting it. I am very much looking forward to the next ... books in the series...!"

Karen Memmott

"I thoroughly enjoyed Celtic Storms and am way past anticipating the second in the series. I have read historical romance for over twenty years and the way the author transformed the genre and included paranormal elements (witchcraft, ESP, druidism, shape-shifting, etc.) was impressive."

S. Sinclaire

I liked the characters a lot, and they seemed well thought-out. The story flowed fairly well, and even included some surprises I didn't see coming! The cliff-hanger ending left me ready for the next book!"

L. Alexander

To my dear friend Tammy,
the strongest woman that I know.

prologue

Burke Lands
Western Ireland
Spring, 1458

Oraeden O'Malley," said a very disgruntled teenaged Orla Burke through clenched teeth, "We should'a been back for the clan games hours ago."

"I know it," he replied, sighing as he sat down with a thump against the cave wall. Running a dirt-covered hand through his unruly hair, he grunted aloud. "I'm almost done here," he added, scratching his forehead. "I am just having trouble with this one thang," he said pointing to a partially worn off wall scraping, a symbol of some kind he supposed.

After having spent the better part of the morning searching through the watery caves that border the shore in Burke territory, Orla was beginning to think they'd never leave her once beloved home-land. Braeden had woken her before sunrise and managed to talk one of the O'Malley clan's shipmasters into taking them up the coast into the realm of Burke territory – home of their now sworn enemies.

Most of the Burke clan had escaped the lands many months back, taking refuge with surrounding clans, Braeden's included. The

O'Malley's even welcomed the infamous Burke witch, Odetta Burke, eldest daughter of the late Burke Laird and the reluctant wife to Easal ~now their worst adversary.Orla's once-upon-a-time *mother*, Odetta Burke, had turned out to actually be her aunt.

It was a risk they took, coming back to the lands where Orla had been raised as the daughter of Odetta. How hard it was for Braeden to forget, he had once been held captive there himself. If it hadn't been for his fiery determination, combat training, and Irish pluck, he might have never escaped.

Why on earth are we here?, thought Orla to herself. "If Easal catches us, we are as good as dead I tell ye," she barked at Braeden to no avail.Orla cringed to think of what her former step-father's reaction would be to finding them on his land. "Tell me again what ye are doin'," she breathed.

"It's a recitation."

"A recitation," she mumbled under her breath, "for what?" she asked.

"To call them forth," he replied matter-of-factly.

"Call what forth?"

"Why – the dragons," he said nonchalantly, "the dragons, of course. Can't ye see the drawings here?" he asked.

Orla rose from her perch against the stony cave wall and ventured to the furthest corner of the cave where Braeden knelt, torch in hand, following the drawings with his finger.

"It's this part, right here," he exclaimed, "that I can't quite figure out. This thang," he pointed. "Do ye ken what this means?" he asked as he traced a cylindrical object which depicted wavy lines cascading around it.

"Aye," she said, crossing her arms and stamping her foot. "I know what it is."

"No, ye, don't," he retorted. "Yer just playing with me. How would ye know anahow?"

"Because I do ye old horses arse," replied Orla. "I've had me training, and I know what it is I tell ye. I've been taught to read the maps."

"Well then smart-breeches, why don't ye tell me then?" he snorted standing up to look her in the eye, albeit on his tip-toes. She was only a few months older than he, but she was a good three inches taller. And that fact, she never tired of reminding him.

"'Tis not a thang, Braeden," she gasped. "'Tis a place."

"What place?"

"Finnegan Falls," he said, "in *O'Malley land*, she snorted pointing behind her towards the south, where they'd come from. Stooping down to get a better look at the drawings, she traced her finger over the outline of the object and gasped. Standing straight upright, she held her left hand over her mouth and gulped. "Braeden," she whispered, "that right there," she pointed, "is Dragon's Point."

one

O'Malley Lands
Western Ireland
The Clan Games

Jamie Burke closed his eyes and prayed. He had counted to three before he opened them. But there was no one there. It was dark, and there was no Daenal standing in the distance. Even though he had been blind since birth, he had the ability to "see" shapes, shadows, and glimpses of light energy which surrounded most living creatures. And right now – he desperately wanted to "see" Daenal O'Malley, the woman he loved and hoped to have a future with.

Oh, how he wished he had not loosed that arrow. It would have been better to have let Daenal go, let her marry the other man, than to risk her life on a risky stunt to prove his manhood. But she was the one that insisted. Archery was the final category in the clan games and Jamie wasn't about to give in or give up or give her over that easily if she didn't want him to. And she didn't want him to. The thought sent blood rushing through his veins, he could feel the warmth grow in his cheeks and he was certain his competitors would mistake his blush for fear.

Their connection was palpable. From the first moment he laid his "eyes" on Daenal, he knew. She was surrounded by an immensely warm glow; he just knew she was the one. The one he had been told about it, the one that would change his life forever. He saw the trusting blue aura surround her when he raised the bow, saw it pulsate a light green when he drew back the line - and he closed his eyes in silent prayer when he loosed it.

Time seemed to literally stand still for a brief moment. He was frozen. His heart beat ferociously in his ears and his hands began to shake. Oh - *what had he done?* His thoughts were soon interrupted by an ominous whirling sound that appeared to grow louder and louder. The pounding of what seemed hundreds of feet against the hard ground beneath him confirmed his suspicions. Something terrible was happening or happened and he was terrified he had missed his mark.

The whirling soon mellowed to a slight hum and he was able to hear voices now. Still searching ahead for his precious Daenal, Jamie made to lurch forward. Abruptly— as he sensed a motion in front of him, he ran towards the target before LordPatrick MacCahan O'Malley raised a hand to stop him.

"Wait," commanded Patrick. "Do'no' move."

It was then that Jamie realized the whirling sound had ceased altogether and had been substituted with the shouts of people fleeing the grounds. There was a commotion beside and behind him, and he felt the thunderous pounding of moving feet.

*What is that smell?*He thought to himself, still being held back by Patrick's determined hand.

"Is that a fire?" Jamie murmured.

"Aye," whispered Patrick, struggling with his dragon-crest ring, which was tightening against his finger. "Now do'no' move, mayhap it willno' see us," he muttered as he bent over attempting again in vain to remove the pinching, glowing ring.

"What?" Jamie whispered back, before noticing that the dark shape between him and Daenal moved. The shape appeared to turn and light up slightly by a brief flash of fire before it stilled, resting directly in front of the men. Waiting.

"Patrick," Jamie asked softly, "Where is Daenal?"

"She is there Jamie, and she is safe," Patrick responded. ""Do'no' move," he repeated.

"Patrick, what is th-that?" he asked. "I canna' see it. There is somethin' jest ahead of us—what is it?"

The smell enveloped Jamie's nostrils again, and he thought he might have recognized the stench as sulfur. *What on earth?* He thought.

Patrick's right hand ceased its burning, and his ring relinquished its tight grip on his finger. Looking down at his hand, he noticed the eyes on the ring were no longer lit up. "Lucian, what do we do?" Patrick asked the robed man to his right.

"Keep still Patrick, and Jamie, quit fidgeting," echoed the elderly scribe's soft reply. "We wait, to see what it wants."

"What it wants?" Jamie asked. "What in god's name is it Patrick?"

"Jamie," Patrick whispered slowly, "'Tis a dragon."

"A dragon?" Jamie repeated under his breath. He had heard tales of such but had never in his life believed them to be true. " living, breathing dragon?" he whispered in astonishment to Patrick.

"A fire-breathing dragon," Patrick corrected as he released his arm from in front of Jamie's chest.

"Fire-breathing ye say?" Jamie asked nervously fiddling with the bow still clutched in his left hand.

"Aye."

"By the gods," Jamie gasped, finally able to make out the outline of a creature standing not more than ten yards before him. It was a clear gold metallic aura he recognized first, muted against the noonday sun until wisps of smoke and fire billowed from its large mouth. In one monumental turn, it rose on its hind legs, stretched out its wings and let out a magnificent cry that sent shivers down his spine.

"Shite," whispered Patrick while Lucian grunted in fear.

"Do no' fear," said Jamie. "He means us no harm."

"How do you know that?" Patrick retorted, clearly un-comforted.

"Aye, how do you know that?" repeated Lucian.

"I can see it," Jamie repeated calmly and slowly as he inched forward toward the dragon. Laying his bow on the ground beside him, he clasped his hands in front of him and began to hum. Soon, his melody was deeper and stronger as Daenal began to chant loudly as well.

"He's calming," remarked Patrick in shock. "He's seated now."

"I'm going in to get a better look," whispered Jamie. He could clearly tell from the outline of the creature that it was tall, probably eight feet or more, nearly two men wide and by the shaking of the ground when it moved, heavy indeed. Its eyes glowed molten amber and the whirling noise evidenced the folding and unfolding of its enormous wings.

"Watch for Daenal, no matter what happens to me, watch for Daenal. Take care of her please, she is me betrothed now. Let no harm come to her."

"Yer the one that said it meant us no harm," Lucian remarked smugly.

"'Tis right ye are, I did say that. I meant, it means us no harm, every time it looks at Daenal, it gets a strange coloring about it and it breathes the fire. I don't rightly know what to make of it. It's as if it's irritated with her for some reason."

"Why would it be irritated by her?" Patrick remarked under his breath. It wasn't as frightening as Patrick would have imagined. It seemed a calm yet regal creature. Strong and steadfast, it held its ground. It obviously had a reason for being here, at this moment in time, but what that reason might be was anybody's guess. It stood there, breathing heavily, staring down the two druid priests; Patrick, the clan's Lord and Lucian, the clan's scribe. And then there was Jamie Burke, Patrick's soon-to-be brother-in-law. The largest man he had ever known and the fiercest warrior in these parts according to rumor and most amazingly, blind since birth. What was Jamie Burke going to do with an angry fire-breathing dragon?

Having, in fact, been the first to win the archery competition in the clan games, Jamie Burke, of the rival Burke clan, would now marry Daenal O'Malley, Patrick's wife's sister. That is if Jamie survived his impending encounter with the dragon, who, it seemed, was intently set on meeting Daenal.

Jamie could see Daenal's aura in the distance change from a calm blue/green hue to the muddled gray of unrepressed fear and panic. "Nochtagh d' ridgefloit," Jamie uttered loudly in the direction of the creature.

Patrick and Lucian exchanged knowing glances and took up the charge behind Jamie, walking in sync with his footsteps. They gasped as the dragon crest rings on their right hands lit up again and burned hot against their skin.

"Nochtagh d' ridgefloit," Jamie repeated more forcefully this time as he came to a stop about twenty feet directly in front of the dragon. "Nichrott," he added.

Instead of calming the creature, Jamie's words appeared to irritate the dragon further and it turned suddenly in the direction of Daenal. There were about thirty yards between the dragon and Daenal and Jamie Burke meant to close that gap as quickly as possible. Would he be any match for its speed?

"What did he say to him?" Patrick asked Lucian in wonder.

"I'm no' sure exactly," Lucian replied, shaking his head. "I am no' at all clear about the language, it sounds something like an ancient dialect I once heard."

"He said, 'She is mine,'" spoke Flynn Montgomery from behind them. "She is mine. Leave her be."

TWO

Dragon's Point

Daenal awoke in a fog. Her head was splitting and she could feel a slight trickle of fresh blood slithering down her cheek. Or was that rain? Or water? She couldn't be sure. It was the noise that was deafening. Slowly, she rose to her feet, pressing her hands against the hard, cold stone wall of what she presumed was some type of cave. She could see the faint outline of muted light in the distance, mere feet in front of her, and she made the light her goal. Inching her way slowly towards the source of it, she lost her footing and tripped over a protruding stone.

"Ouch," she muttered under her breath before regaining her composure and taking up her quest once again. She cursed her long flaxen hair before tying it in a hasty knot at the nape of her neck. Thankful she had worn her truis and deerskin boots, she tied the bottom of her tunic around her waist and stood straight up to get a better eye on her footing. She didn't want to trip again so, she would have to be very careful. And this time, time she would work more slowly.

It was dusk by now and the light she thought she saw was actually a reflection of the moon against the backdrop of the bay surrounding O'Malley port. *How high up am I?* She thought to herself. Another cold drop of liquid cascaded across her forehead and she realized at once it was water hitting her head, not blood. *Thank the gods*, was her first reaction, before pure panic took over when she realized she must be high above the cliffs near Dragon's Point, the plateaued ridge adjacent to Finnegan Falls.

The Falls! How in the world would she have gotten up to the Falls? It was near impossible to traverse the grounds on foot, let alone climb the twenty foot rock wall leading to the mouth of the cave which sat behind the waterfall, overlooking the port. Her head swam again and she caught a whiff of what smelled like burning flesh or burnt food or – could it be – sulfur?

The legends surrounding Dragon's Point were many and varied. They had been passed down from generation to generation, throughout the village and neighboring clans. As far as she could recall, no one in her lifetime had ever traversed the ledge she now stood on. Looking over the falls, she imagined how cold the violently running water might be. How long the fall would take if she were to step out, and if her spine would simply snap in two upon impact or if anyone could possibly survive such a violent descent. *How could they?* She breathed to herself.

After giving her physical senses liberty to distinguish her surroundings, she realized there was something else that she was missing. There in the back of her sub-conscious was a nagging sensation. It began as a forlorn melancholy hum and grew stronger, darker, deeper and foreboding. It was unmistakable. Sickness or injury, she was surrounded by the despair of weakness, of un-wholeness. So much, so that she became nauseated and shaky. She began to weep.

There was stillness in the air, the kind that only came with the realization of the presence of dis-ease. Someone was desperately in need of healing and she could feel it. Was that why she had been brought here? Had someone taken her and brought her - here? How on earth did they get up the side of the rock wall? The humming in her ears grew stronger, yet – it wasn't the sound of the falls that she was hearing. It was as if her heart was beating so loudly within her chest that it had infested her mind, like a hundred drummers pounding in synchronicity. Looking down at her hands, she realized she was injured. There were scratch marks and dried blood trailing along her forearm, down towards her wrists.

For a moment, she thought she might faint, but she steeled herself and began controlled breathing, just like the elder scribe, Airard, had instructed her. Had it not been for the controlled breathing, she would never have made it to through the clan games or offered to hold that apple during the archery contest. *The contest! Oh my, what had become of Jamie?*

A rustling behind her brought to memory the activities of the day. The clan celebrations, the contests, and Jamie, her beloved, as he pulled back the arrow. And - the terrible, winsome noise with the thunderous landing made by *that creature.* The unmistakable look of horror on Jamie's face, Patrick and Lucian's equaled panic and her sister, Darina. Darina was plump and round with her first child which was due in only a few weeks. She was clearly very concerned and she was also confused and obviously angry with her and Jamie both.

"What kind of stunt de ye think yer pulling here, me seesta?" Darina asked. But Daenal had no real answer. Darina wasn't the type to understand Daenal's 'feelings', instead chalking her "gifts" up to superstition and childlike imaginations. The worst fights and misunderstandings she could ever recall Darina having with their mother had been over Daenal and "her ways." In the end, mother had always won out, and Darina had learned to bite her tongue, but when it came to the survival of the clan, Darina was not so forgiving. As the eldest daughter of Dallin O'Malley, Darina took her responsibilities seriously. Now that she was the Laird's wife and second in command, she was a force to be reckoned with.

Agreeing to allow Jamie Burke to compete in the games against the other sighted suitors may have seemed a good idea at first. He was, after all, better with a sword than any of the others, a good two heads and shoulders above the rest, and strong as an ox. He wasn't. However, a keen archer, having been blind since birth. Daenal had to admit it was a risk letting him raise a bow in her direction.

It was at that moment, when the arrow was loosed that her world seemed to stand perfectly still. Nothing could have frightened or excited her more; the prospect of becoming wife to Jamie Burke, or by that marriage, becoming the wife of the new Burke clan leader. That is after Jamie claimed his rightful place from Easal. War would ensue, of that she had no doubt. But it had to happen. Jamie would regain the territory from the rogue leader and the Burke tribes would return to their own lands in time.   It was Jamie's mother that frightened her most.

Odetta Burke had a long history of scuffles with the O'Malley clan and worst of all she was known as an evil witch. Would Daenal's own spiritual gifts be any match for Odetta's black magic? What part would Jamie's own relationship with his new-found mother play in the Burke uprising? The weeks and months to come seemed to vanish from her purview as she recalled her current circumstances. High above the port, she stood and prayed for clarity. Breathing deeply, she caught the smell of fresh blood in her nostrils and at once realized it was not her own. In fact, it didn't seem to be human at all.

Daenal's meditations were interrupted sadly by visions of her betrothed, Jamie Burke. *Her Jamie*. The kindest, the noblest man she had ever known. Her *champion*. He had so valiantly played in the clan games and even won her hand by winning the archery competition.

But at what cost? Where was he now? Where was she and how would he ever find her?

"The Lord will see you *now*," the sentry murmured in her direction. "And bring the scrolls, he says." Turning to avert his eyes, Ochnar silently pitied the woman. She wasn't really a prisoner per se, but she wasn't free to leave Burke castle. A *permanent guest* more aptly described the situation. It had been months, and still she remained. Easal made sure she was made comfortable, but was clear that she would remain until he had want he wanted. And what he wanted was the impossible. Naelyn knew she would never leave.

She rose from her red satin covered bed and donned the closest thing within reach, a thin linen shift. Taking the candle at her bedside, she lit the lantern sitting atop the dressing table. She turned towards the wardrobe against the far wall and chose a green dressing robe. Splashing water on her face, she noted her reflection in the looking glass - the lines had grown deeper and her eyes had grown hollow. She had grown accustomed to the strange hours that Easal kept and adjusted her schedule accordingly. She slept during the day, and she "worked" at night. He seemed to always call for her once the sun set and her face was wearing the results of her interrupted sleep patterns.

She let out a helpless, hopeless sigh before struggling with her slippers and standing upright, straightening her robe.

"Ochnar," she half whispered, half mumbled, "The Lord has the key to the chest."

"Aye," he grunted before turning around to face her. "Aye, I remember," he nodded his head in aggravation. "I will return shortly, milady," he said before bowing and backing his way out of what used to be the Lady of the Castle's personal chamber.

Odetta's chamber was the most unusual in the entire Burke fortress. Unique was the best word to describe it because Odetta was, well - a unique individual. Although the appointments were lavish and beautiful, they were interlaced with unusual relics and interesting artifacts. Odetta had begun collecting weapons, scientific tools and some utterly bizarre things in her early youth. Much to her father's chagrin, her mother had supported her perplexing curiosity and enabled many of her most delicate purchases. Executioner's swords, guillotine blades, surgical instruments, ancient texts, rock carvings and religious inscriptions. It was the looking glass collection that Odetta prized beyond all others. After her father's death, she was finally able to replace some of the looking glasses he had shattered in his many fits of rage. Her mother made certain she was educated beyond necessity for her station in life.

It was just this curiosity and her interest in celestial bodies that qualified Odetta as the most learned expert on the stars in all of Burke Lands. It's what made her chamber in the Burke Castle the most unusual - *Odetta's Sky,* as it was called. That's what was interesting about this particular chamber in Burke Castle.

That's what kept Naelyn up at night. It was hard to sleep when the universe literally stared at you from above. Odetta had managed to completely recreate the night sky in the domed ceiling of her monstrous chamber. On the southeast wall were intricate dates and calendars depicting moon cycles, eclipses, meteor showers and even some compelling weather prophesies. No one understood how Odetta knew, she just did. And - she was rarely wrong. Even when she *was* wrong, she was *still right*, she was just early - her mother would say, "Patience is not her virtue."

Naelyn was bone tired. Tired of searching the scrolls for answers for Easal when there were none, and especially tired of spending her days tirelessly struggling for the benefit of others. She was tired and she knew that she would remain tired and die tired and have nothing to show for her tired, miserable life.

She was a prisoner, but she had always been a prisoner really. Born poor and orphaned at an early age, she worked vigorously for the nuns in the fields and all she got was one meal and a dirty cot for her efforts. When Odetta rescued her during the raids on the church and monastery, she had taken pity on her and cared for her. It wasn't the care a mother would provide, but it was better than one meal a day and a dirty cot.

She taught her as well, to read, to decipher to exchange money, all of the things a high-born lady would know. And she had trusted her. Odetta wasn't many things, but loyal was one of them. Once you earned Odetta's respect, you were something and somebody and by virtue of association, you were to be respected. She was her maker. Without Odetta, Naelyn would most probably be dead by now or working in some filthy brothel or worse.

But that was before and this was now and things were much, much different.

"Are ye coming?" asked Ochnar from the entry way.

"Aye," she said turning away from the looking glass. The moon greeted her bright and full from beyond the far window pain, and Naelyn knew without a doubt, it would be a long, tiring night.

Orla and Braeden continued their trek through the high marsh just this side of the Rocky shoreline along the coast of Burke lands. It had become quite clear that their boatman left them with no intention of ever returning. Thankfully Orla's ranting diminished to a simple small whimper here and there. Exhaustion had taken hold and pain had replaced her fear for a moment. There was now a large hole in the bottom of her left boot and a blister was wearing through. But that was nothing compared to the knot growing on the back of her head. Slipping on that large rock sent her flying and Braeden felt terrible and small that he was unable to reach her before she landed.

"Tell me again where it is ye are taking me," Orla demanded, rubbing the top of her head with her left hand.

Braeden let out a long, aggravated sigh and turned around to face her. Gripping her by the shoulders, he looked stern and straight into her eyes, "Orla. Have ye lost yer wits? I know ye hit yer head, but I've told ye this going on three times now. Just up the way a bit," he exclaimed cocking his head to the left. "There is an old hollowed out tree trunk. It should provide enough cover for tonight and disguise the fire. On the morrow, we will get and up and hike our way back to the O'Malley keep."

He could see the tears pooling in Orla's eyes. Now that did it. He couldn't take that. Her crystal blue eyes filled with tears, and that made him want to cry too. But he couldn't, he wouldn't, and he wasn't he had to be strong. It wasn't that the boatman left that scared him the most. It's what they had found in the caves, the drawings, they pulled him in and spoke of what was to come and that frightened him more than anything in the world.

Grabbing her left hand forcefully, Braeden pulled them forward through the high marsh, deeper into the forest. The tree trunk was nearly three miles south, but he wouldn't tell Orla. If she had any idea how far they had to go, she would have given up already. He wasn't altogether certain she would make it, but he knew he could carry her if he had to and that would be no chore. Orla was not only his best friend in the entire world, she was the toughest, most stubborn, and the most aggravating person he'd ever known. Together, anything was possible.

With a loud cry, Orla grabbed at her left foot and sunk to the ground with a thud.

"Whatever do ye think ye are doing Orla?" Braeden cried. "We 'aven't the time to stop. We 'ave to keep going."

The tears were flowing fiercely now and Orla would soon be inconsolable. He watched as she jerked and tugged and finally removed her left boot. Her foot was bleeding because of the hole in the bottom of her boot. Her boot had ruptured the blister. "I think it will be easier to go without me boots," she said, between whimpers, "This boot is killing me."

Bending down to take a better look, Braeden saw the damage that had been caused. It wasn't a serious injury, but it would be enough to slow them down. "Orla," said Braeden, "I know yer foot hurts and I'm sorry, but we 'ave to keep going." Orla shook her head in resistance and wiped her tears with the back of her right hand. "Orla," Braeden said again, "I can help you."

"I don't need any help Braeden," Orla said through clenched teeth.

"Yer clearly in pain," he remarked, "We 'ave to keep moving. I can carry ye. Ye know that I can." Orla grew quiet. The tears had stopped and instead been replaced with shivers, the night was unfolding, the temperature had dropped and it was starting to lightly mist. Before long, it would be raining out right, and they would be in trouble. Indeed, if they didn't reach their tree in time, they would be in grave danger.

Braeden ripped the sleeve from his left arm and tied it carefully around Orla's injured foot. She watched but said nothing alarmed at the amount of sensitivity he displayed having never seen such tenderness before. Braeden wasn't exactly a hardened individual, he was more no-nonsense, practical, straightforward, and in many ways closed off. His life experiences had left him that way, as had Orla's.

Lifting her chin with his right hand, Braeden looked directly into her eyes. "Orla, I'm going to pick ye up. There is nothing that ye can do about it. We have to make it to the tree before it starts raining or else ye'll catch yer death of cold. I'm not going to argue with ye about this, ye might as well give up now."

Orla smiled and nodded her head. It wasn't often that she was left speechless. But Braeden had made his intentions clear and she was in no mood to fight him. He simply sighed and smiled back disbelievingly. *Just imagine what could happen if we worked together,* he thought to himself. Braeden jerked his head upright, indicating it was time to go. Orla obligingly wrapped her arms around his neck and waited for him to lift her. It was effortless. She knew Braeden was strong, but she had no idea just how strong. She caught a whiff of his scent at the back of his neck where his hair nuzzled her nose, and she knew immediately she was in deep trouble.

three

O'Malley Keep

lord Patrick O'Malley and his Scottish cousin on his mother's side, Flynn Montgomery, traversed a long and winding tunneled stairway below the great clan hall in O'Malley Castle side-by-side. They exchanged knowing looks and sighed in unison. Flynn adjusted the torch in his right hand before smoothing his long hair at the nape of his neck.

"How is Darina?" Flynn ventured hesitantly.

"She is resting now," replied Patrick, remarkably without the stutter he had carried since adolescence. "She very nearly exhausted herself and me in the process with her rantings about the games," he added.

"Patrick, have ye ever seen a dragon afore?" asked Flynn.

"Nay, can't say as I 'ave."

"What do ye think caused it to - uh - um - appear then? Reckon someone beckoned it?" asked Flynn.

"Beckoned it?" replied Patrick, before stopping mid-step and turning to face Flynn. "Jest what do ye know about dragons Flynn?"

"Not much, I must admit," he responded holding his hands out as if in surrender, "but me mam did speak of 'em from time and again."

"And – what would yer mam know about dragons Flynn?" Patrick asked accusingly.

"Well, she came from a long line of Dragonians. She wore a molten ring, just like ye do Patrick," he added, pointing to the dragon crest symbol on a silver ring on Patrick's right hand. "Yer ring, it grew hot and lit up just afore the dragon appeared, did it no'?" he inquired.

"Aye, it did." Patrick tipped his head to the side in contemplation, holding his hand out in front of him to get a better look at the ring. Shaking his head, he lowered his hand back to his side and leaned against the cavernous wall. "I was given the ring when me mam died. I was told it made *me* a Dragonian, although I've never truly understood what that means."

"Lucian has a similar ring, does he no'? asked Flynn.

"He does."

"Where did he get his ring?" he asked before sitting down on the last stair leading to the council chamber's corridor.

"His older brother, Airard, sent it to him last year. Had it sent over from MacCahan lands, my family's clan, just before I arrived here to wed Darina? Airard told Lucian he would explain all things to him in due time."

"Well, Patrick," said Flynn as he arose from his seat on the stairs and took up step with Patrick down the corridor. "I believe due time is come," he added motioning for Patrick to enter the council chamber before him.

Lucian greeted him at the door, a preemptive strike it seemed, because close behind him stood Darina. The elder scribe had a look of pure mental exhaustion on his face. Patrick could definitely relate, and he could also sympathize. Swollen with their first child, Darina's nerves had been on edge for quite some time. Considering the tragic events surrounding her sister Daenal's capture by the dragon, any mood she would be in would be understandable.

"Patrick," greeted Airard from the far right corner of the Council Chamber. It had been several months since Patrick had seen his mentor, Airard. He arrived only days earlier from Patrick's homeland. It was indeed good to see him. Surely Airard would know what to do, if anyone on the face of the earth would know it would be he. Lucian's older brother was in declining health and Patrick silently suspected this visit was partly to say his goodbyes.

"Airard my dear friend," Patrick said, clearly.

Patrick hadn't stuttered once in some time, not since the day that Daenal prayed with him. Patrick had invoked his own healing, she assured him. Of that, he was thankful. It certainly made communication easier and quicker, but he often wondered why the injury to his right arm could not be healed in the same manner.

"I am so glad you're here," Patrick whispered as he hugged Darina about the waist carefully searching for a tiny kick or bump. He motioned for Darina to sit next to his seat at the Council table, before taking his own seat next to her. Reaching across the table, he grabbed a pitcher and poured a small glass of elderberry wine and set it before her, hoping the spirits would calm her nerves.

"Patrick," began Lucian, "We are only waiting for one other person."

"Jamie, I presume,?" asked Patrick.

"Aye," said Gemma. "We had to send a sentry out to get him, he was half way to Burke lands with his guards. It took them quite a while to convince him to come back, but they managed. I assume he'll be in no kind of mood when he arrives," she murmured.

"Could ye blame him?" asked Darina with a thick Irish brogue. "Me seesta has been gone for several hours and nothings been done about it."

Galen spoke up, "Darina. What we have is very delicate situation that has to be handled in a very delicate way." The priest spoke in a very calm manner, hoping his words would provide some type of comfort to Darina. "I think we may have an unconventional solution..."

"Let's not go and get ahead of ourselves," interrupted Darina's uncle Ruarc. "What we need to do is wait on Jamie, before anything else is said."

"And why is that?" Darina demanded. "Daenal has only been Jamie's betrothed for a short time, she has been me seesta for seventeen years. Right now, she could be dead. And we would not know it because no one budged, not even one finger has been lifted to do anything about this."

"I wouldn't say no one," interrupted Jamie Burke from the entrance to the Council Chamber. Followed by his guards, Jamie was an imposing figure indeed. Tall, muscular, with ruddy good looks, he could arouse fear and curiosity simply with his presence. His marble-like blue eyes added to the mystery. Everyone knew he was blind since birth, but he had a way of navigating that made it appear as if he was fully sighted. Jamie's ability to read auras left him with no handicap. In fact, Jamie was probably a better judge of character than anyone. After all, it was hard to hide your energy and seldom did anyone's intentions go unnoticed by Jamie Burke.

'Would ye please explain to me why me and me guards were stopped?" Jamie shouted thunderously into the center of the room, to anyone and everyone all at the same time. His voice was authoritative and determined and there was no doubt he meant to be taken seriously.

Patrick rose from his seat and reached a hand towards Jamie, who promptly accepted it. "Jamie won't ye please have a seat?" asked Patrick. Obliging him, Jamie walked to the back of the Council Chamber and sat in his newly established position at the table. As the heir to the Burke clan Lordship, Jamie had become the leader of the Burke refugees now living in O'Malley territory. Patrick made him a member of the O'Malley Council the moment he expressed his desire to wed Daenal.

"I think we're all here," said Galen from his perch at the scribe's table in the corner of the room. "Ruarc, Lucian, Airard, Jamie, Gemma, Darina and, oh - Kurt couldn't make it."

"Let us begin," Patrick said. I've had a discussion with Gemma earlier about some matters that the Council may need to be aware of. These things may have some bearing on how we can help Daenal."

"Help Daenal?", interrupted Jamie. "I was on my way to get Daenal back and yer sentry stopped me!"

"Jamie," spoke Airard softly from across the table, "I believe something very important is about to be said and I think we all would like to hear it. Can you give Gemma just a moment of yer time?"

"Would this have anything to do with Gemma being a shifter?" Jamie asked.

Darina gasped, placing her right hand over her mouth and her left hand on her protruding belly, "What do ye mean she's a shifter?"

Lucian stood up, wrapping his fingertips atop the Council table. "Jamie," he asked, "what makes ye think Gemma is a shifter?"

Galen, who had stopped taking notes moments before, stood as well. As did Ruarc, but Airard snickered under his breath, "I'm sure it's quite evident to Master Burke." He said chuckling again, this time his shoulders visibly shaking.

"Patrick," exclaimed Darina, "What does this mean? Shifter- what do ye mean?" she repeated directing her question to Jamie.

Gemma interrupted, "Jamie's right, I am a shifter and I think I can help find Daenal."

"I don't need any *help* finding Daenal," stated Jamie, matter-of-factly. "In fact, I think we all know where she's been taken. The only question is whether or not it's too late."

"Well. Where is she," asked Darina. "If we know where she is, why haven't we gotten her?"

Jamie grunted, an *I told you so* kind of reminder that this is exactly what he was on his way to do. "Well, unless you can climb Finnegan falls, I'm quite certain you won't be able to bring her back."

Darina gasped and her uncle Ruarc continued, "that's right Dragon's Point. I realize none of us ever really believed in dragons, but after what happened, we've got no choice. And we can only assume the Dragon would take her to its lair, which happens to be high atop the port at Finnegan Falls."

"But what has that to do with Gemma?" questioned Darina.

Jamie and Lucian spoke in unison. "Show her."

Gemma rose and giving a reluctant sigh removed her cloak and handed it to Airard to her right. "Would ye hold on to this for me?" she asked

Gemma was a lovely woman, not only was she the elected leader of the Island of Women, but she was one of the most respected women in all of O'Malley clan. She had always been an O'Malley clan member, having come at an early age with her mother, a transplant from the McAllister clan just North of Burke lands. In her early forties, Gemma had beautiful champagne-colored hair with just a hint of gray and beautiful gray eyes to match. She was quite possibly the most intelligent woman Patrick had ever met. Besides his mother, that was, and his cunning wife.

Never married, Gemma was content to raise her family on her own. Her youngest, a girl, was just under 10 months. Gemma earned her position in the clan and with the women on the island the old-fashioned way; through hard work, determination and a keen sense of fairness and justice. Although she was trustworthy and respected, she was also closed off and very private. Not many knew the private Gemma, and what they were about to learn would shock them to their cores.

FOUR

Dragon's Point

her head was spinning, her stomach growling and her back was painfully aware of her predicament. It took a few moments for Daenal to realize just where she was. How on earth had she managed to fall asleep under such circumstances? She was normally vigilant, observant and highly intuitive. However, the events of the past few weeks had proven to her in no uncertain terms that she was in fact *human*. Not that she ever believed she was anything more than fallible; she had always been able to maintain her composure in a crisis, as well as maintain a cool head.

Here she was high above the O'Malley port, a prisoner of some sort, to a creature she knew very little about. Other than the legends and tales that had been passed down from generation to generation, dragons were a virtual unknown to Daenal. She must've passed out while in the dragon's clutches. Finnegan falls was only a few miles from where the games were being held. It wouldn't have taken very long for them to arrive at the cave opening. No doubt being unconscious was a mercy to her. Her fear of heights would have gotten the better of her anyway.

It didn't take very long for Daenal to realize she was not alone. Something was snoring or groaning in the back of the cave. There was the stench of fish in the air and the loud falling of the water sent her senses into overload. She wondered for a moment how long she had been there, was she the first human to arrive? Had she any hope of escape or was she destined to starve to death or worse, become food for the creature. But if she were to become food for the creature, why wasn't she already dead?

It was all coming back to her now. *The games.* Her Jamie! Oh, what had become of her Jamie? She saw the look of fear in his eyes. Those eyes, those beautiful crystalline eyes that saw right through to her soul.He had charged the beast! It wasn't fear in his eyes. It was pure rage! It was ownership and fierce indignation that possessed him at that moment; she was his and nothing and no one, not even a Dragon, would keep them apart.

Her head was spinning again. She reached up to clutch each side. Gripping the tips of her ears she massaged them the way that her mother taught her. It did nothing to quell the headache that had come upon her. That noise. Here it was again a whirling, whistling, whining type noise that could only mean one thing.The Dragon was on its way back and what on earth would she do?`

Even above the loud falling water, she could make out the unmistakable sound of Dragon's wings. A high pierced cry from the back of the cave sent shivers up her spine. Feeling her way in the semi-darkness; she etched the cold, cavernous walls with her left hand, creeping slowly towards the cave entrance and a large rock where she hoped she could hide. Mindful of her footing, she was grateful she had worn her boots and truis, rather than the traditional game gown worn by Laird's daughters.

Daenal had grown accustomed to maneuvering in the dark. Her older sister would not have approved, but she had spent the better part of the last few evenings exploring the shoreline with her beloved Jamie. They knew they were meant for one another and were intent on getting to know one another better before the wedding. She was safe enough with Jamie, the fiercest warrior in all the land. It was her virtue her sister would be concerned with and with appearances. Not that anyone would ever question Daenal's purity, her integrity was something she valued, above all else. It was the fact that the elder sons from all the surrounding clans were there to compete for her hand. To give the impression that she was less than noble in the presence of Jamie Burke could pose a problem for them all.

She moved close against the wall of the cave, careful to make as little noise as possible until she reached the jutting rock. She fit just behind it, almost as if it were created and situated there just for her. It was dark and the shadows cast about the cavern further disguised her presence. She knew the dragon could most likely smell her, and it would also know she had nowhere to go, but right now, she had no intention of being the focus of attention. Especially since whatever was in the back of the cave, was moving towards her now, towards the mouth of the cave, no doubt to meet the dragon upon its arrival.

It had to be another dragon, although her senses told her it was small and most likely ill. Her gift was sometimes a curse, and she knew that whatever it was, it was not whole, it was suffering and it needed help. Was this why she had been brought here? Had the dragon sensed somehow that Daenal could assist with healing? *Surely not. These barbaric creatures couldn't have that kind of intuition.*

The loudest screech she had ever heard announced the arrival of the dragon that had taken her. The brush of its wings against the falling water sent sprays of liquid in every direction, soaking the ground in the cave, the walls and Daenal in the process. Yet, she remained still and soundless. She wiped back a loose sprig of drenched hair to clear her vision.

A thud felt under her feet alerted her that the space she shared with the "other" was closing in. It was half-running, falling, tumbling in her direction. Her blood pressure shot up and the hair on the back of her neck straightened as if drawn away by some magnetic force.

It returned with a loud screeching sound, and tumbled, head over feet, over wings, towards the mouth of the cave, nearly falling over the side into the waterfall, before being caught up in the wings of the elder Dragon. Daenal watched in awe as the creatures greeted each other warmly. The large dragon was visibly affectionate with the smaller, and the smaller dragon was clearly dependent and clinging to the older. It was then she noticed something in the clutches of the older dragon's talons. It was a large hare, food for its offspring, she presumed. Before thinking, Daenal let out a loud sigh of relief, perhaps she wouldn't become a meal, after all.

Or would she? It only took a moment to forget where she was. Only one moment to make a simple sound in the wrong place. Only one moment before she was standing face to face, and looking into the glowing red eyes of the largest, most frightening creature she had ever encountered. The earth swam beneath her feet, and Daenal closed her eyes, afraid to imagine what would happen next.

She could feel the rough calluses on his left hand as it followed the line of her spine from top to bottom. The night air was cool, but the fire kept the simple cottage warm enough. Incense burned from atop the side table and her breath blew visibly, moist air mixed with the remnants of the last of the red wine they had shared. She sighed a most contented sigh and rolled over to look her lover in the eye. Sweeping her long black hair behind her, she pulled the thin linen bed sheet up and around her bosom and shivered for dramatic affect.

"Kurt," she whispered, "Aren't ye needed at the council meeting?"

"Aye," he replied softly, as he kissed her on the forehead. "But I ken they can wait a bit yet," he chuckled as he playfully tugged at the sheet which was tucked tightly under her arms.

"Kurt," she repeated, mockingly slapping away his hands in protest. "Ye'll wear me out mon. Are ye making up for lost time?" she teased.

"Aye, I reckon so," the former priest bantered back at her. "But can ye blame me, me love? Ye denied me ever so many years ye see. And for what?" he asked, tipping his nose down and tightening his forehead to make it appear he was most definitely serious.

"Kurt," she replied, "ye know why as well as I do. And for heaven's sake, ye were a Catholic priest!"

"Say it one more time, love, before I go," he pleaded. "Ye know I need to hear it again." This time his voice took on a different tone. It was melancholy and low, almost desperate. She knew she would never be able to make up for the lost time or the heartache she had caused him. She also knew he had forgiven her, long ago. Perhaps even before some of the treacherous and horribly traumatic events of her life had unfolded, engulfing everyone around her, even those she had dared to love in secret.

"I love ye Kurt, I always have." A tear threatened to spill down her cheeks, but he caught it with his thumb and wiped it gently away.

"I'll be back as soon as I can, love. I don't think this should take very long. There isn't much help I can be when it comes to the business of dragons."

"No doubt they will want to question me as well," she added. Her blood pressure shot up at the thought of being brought before the council again. How many times could she explain her situation, what had happened and beg for forgiveness, clemency, mercy even? How could she convince them that she wasn't really the person they thought she was? She had been a victim of circumstance and a tool for an evil, depraved individual from whom she was lucky to have escaped. But for now, she was the scapegoat, the whipping boy, the one person everyone could place their hatred upon justifiably in their minds and for now she would just have to let that be.

She had Kurt, and that was more heaven than she ever thought she would see. They were to be married, as soon as he had secured a cottage of their own, and she would try beyond words to make a life with him. A life. The thought of being married and having a home and maybe children, even at her age, as boring as that sounded, was like a sweet melody to her ears. For all the adventure, she had experience prior had brought heartache and trauma. She patiently waited for the day when those past events were no longer at the forefront of her mind. She knew she could somehow forgive and forget, she just wasn't so sure her new community could do the same.

She saw the looks, heard the murmuring and knew what was thought of her. Kurt assured her that all would be alright, but she wasn't yet convinced. She still feared for her safety, and nightmares overtook her at night. Sleep was nearly impossible, except when Kurt was there, and that had to be in secret. Only her guard knew and she had a sneaking suspicion that wouldn't last long. Kurt said that healing was possible and Daenal may have been the one person in the world that could help her with that. But, now she was gone, perhaps dead, lord knows what had happened to her after the dragon got her in its clutches.

She grasped each side of the face of her dearest friend and pulled him close to her mouth. "I will always love ye, Kurt," she whispered into his mouth as she kissed him, "ye are a gift from the gods."

"I'm not sure the church would agree with ye," he chuckled in response. "I must get," he added, rising from the straw mattress in the corner of the cottage and donning his over cloak. "I'll be back as soon as I can. Until then, yer guard is here. Don't' go anawhere unless ye have to and don't go alone if ye must go."

She nodded in agreement, wiping a stray tear from her cheek. "I shall miss ye," she added, smiling up at him and clutching the wine bottle tightly in her fist. "Can I finish this in yer absence Kurt?"

"But, of course, love," he said, before kneeling down to kiss the top of her forehead. Turning towards the cottage door, he grabbed his knapsack and slung it over his shoulder before signaling her guard to permit him leave. In just a moment, he was gone, into the night, leaving her to contemplate all of the plans they had made for the future – together. And she truly hoped they would have one. She knew she had a future, she was assured of that when the visitor cursed her to immortality. She just wasn't sure if she would share it with anyone who could love her.

five

Burke Territory

ut where on earth are we going?" asked Naelyn, gripping tightly to the lanthorn thrust in her hand by the garish looking guard. She followed him down past the stables, past the brook and towards the north clearing through knee high brush, stony ground, and mire. Losing her footing, she slipped and would have toppled forward had the man not grabbed her by the elbow, stabilizing her gait. "I was to meet with Lord Easal and bring the scrolls," she continued. "Lord Easal will be verra angry I'm, I do ..."

"Hold yer tongue, milady," came the stern reply. "Lord Easal has requested yer assistance and will be meeting us *there*," he stuttered in broken Gaelic.

"*There?*" Naelyn asked. "Where is *there?*"

He eyed her curiously, looking her up and down and around with puzzlement. As if he wondered himself what on earth he was bringing her *there* for. She was just a might of a lass. Barely five feet tall, tiny really, with light, long blonde hair, crystal gray eyes, and wrists the size of a twig. He couldn't imagine why Easal would want her there himself.

"To the catacombs," he replied, matter-of-factly.

"The catacombs," she whispered in fear, before turning around and running as fast as her little legs would carry her. She managed to make it approximately ten yards before her chaperone realized she wasn't following him any longer. It was dark and she needed the lanthorn for sight, but she also knew it would give away her position. Quickly, she blew it out and tossed it as far to her right as she could, it landed without much of a thud.

She stood perfectly still for a moment and let her heart beat catch up with her mind. Gazing straight up at the full moon, she took several deep breaths, all the while hearing the sound of heavy boot steps behind her from the right. She knew she had a good ten seconds before the man would catch up with her. She also knew she would not rot in the catacombs, nor would she become a surrogate mother to Easal's devil child. She had no choice but to escape this man, and she had to be smart about how she did it.

Pulling off her cloak, she threw it to her left. She threw her boots as well, one to the front and the other to the back of her; and quickly climbed the nearest tree she could find. She was an expert climber; something that had become necessary as a child. Drunken men who follow little girls into the woods cannot climb trees, and they have little patience for waiting them out either. The morning would find her alone in the tree and mayhap then she could escape Easal for good, mayhap she could find refuge in O'Malley Lands as well.

As she finally settled in on a thick limb about ten feet up, she realized she was not alone in the tree. Her heartbeat quickened and she began to sweat. Her pulse pounded in her ears and her hands began to shake with the reality of her situation.

"Milady," the rough male voice sounded below her. "I've no intention of spending the entire night here at the foot of this tree. "I intend to take ye to the catacombs where ye have been summoned by Lord Easal."

She gasped for breath as the hissing sound grew louder. The snake had taken up her scent and was slowly making its way in her direction.

"I'd rather suffer this venom than spend me last days in the catacombs," she whispered as loudly as she could.

"Milady," the Lord requests yer presence in the catacombs to assist with an unusual matter that he believes you may be – uh - suited towards."

"What?" she asked. "I am not to become a prisoner?"

"Nay."

"I don't believe ye," she replied. "Why are ye chasing me then?"

"Milady, 'tis a full moon. The dearg-due are out, the wolves are a 'howling and you are my charge," he said with the most unusual accent she had ever heard. "If'n you would but remain stationed there and breathe only if necessary, I think I can impale that serpent with my arrow."

He was right, she really didn't want to become dinner for wolves or worse yet, be drained of all her blood by some she-devil dearg' du. But, the most obvious current problem was the serpent.

The serpent, she remembered. It was now just inches from her, she watched as its glowing yellow eyes floated atop the tree limb in her direction. Slowly it inched its way towards her, never looking away. It was almost hypnotizing the way it locked gazes with her as if it was preparing to be her, to become her somehow. She breathed in slowly and exhaled even more slowly.

"Aye," she moaned, a small verbal acknowledgment that she was indeed at the mercy of the soldier, and whatever her fate, she no longer had control of what became of her.

She had heard the arrow before she saw it strike. A clean whirling sound, a "whoosh", and in a flash the arrow pierced the neck of the rising serpent and sent it plummeting off of the tree limb and onto the woodland floor below her. Thank the gods, he was a good shot. She let out a breath of air and slumped against a tree, wiping the pent up tears with the back of her right hand.

"Do I need to come up there and get you?" he asked abrasively.

"Nay," she said quietly. "I just need a moment, please," she begged. "I won't run, I promise. "Pray tell me," she asked the soldier, "what exactly awaits me at the catacombs?"

She could tell from his lack of immediate response and the aggravated sigh he let out that he wasn't too keen on talking about it. He reached up his hand towards her in beckoning. "We must be off now," he said, more gently than anything that had escaped his pursed mouth so far. "Let's go lass."

As she made her way down the face of the tree, she almost imagined she saw fear and pity in his eyes. She couldn't be sure, but it was the closest thing to sympathy she had ever encountered in her life. What on earth had Easal opened the catacombs for? They had been closed for nearly two hundred years since before the slave trade ended, since before the Romans came, before the Church even.

"Please, tell me," she begged as she climbed into the arms of the sentry. "Wouldn't ye want to know?"

"I reckon as much," he replied as he set her down gently on the damp leaves. "Here," he added shoving her boots in her hands, "Put these on."

"I've no idea what ye call it," he said in broken Gaelic. "The word, I've no confidence I have the right word," he added reluctantly.

Roman, he was Roman. That's why she could barely understand him. A hired soldier for Easal since most of the Burke clan had taken up refuge in O'Malley lands. "It?" she asked. "It's an *it* then?"

"Aye," he replied and nodded at the same time.

"Is it a relic?" she asked, hoping Easal had finally located the Nexus he had been searching for and with it, he would soon be leaving.

"Nay," he replied.

"Is it a scroll? A writing perhaps? On the wall?"

"Nay," he replied, scratching his beard and looking puzzled.

"Hmm," he moaned. "Tis alive."

Dear god she thought to herself, there are more of them! Another Easal or Eaton, a creature from another time and place like the mad monster who held her captive. "Another, Easal?" she gasped.

"Nay, milady," he signed. "'Tis, uh – well – uh – 'tis *il drago*."

"Drago?" she muttered. "Drago? What on earth? Il drago?" she asked turning her head up at the giant of a man before her. "Il drago?"

Clearly aggravated, the century bade her to move forward. Quickly he retrieved the lantern and had it lit. "We must go now."

"Wait, I need to know, please," she begged. "What am I walking into?"

"Il Drago," he repeated, clearly aggravated. "Il Drago," He said it again as he spread his arms up and wide and made flying gestures before crouching down before her and blowing his breath out slowly. "Il Drago."

"A dragon?" she gasped disbelievingly. "A dragon?"

"Ah – dragon," he repeated, clearly proud of himself. "Aye, a dragon," he said turning around to face her, but she was gone. "Naelyn," he called softly. He turned right and she wasn't there, he turned left and she wasn't there either. He made a circle with the lanthorn, but she was gone. She had vanished into thin air! He widened his circle, swinging the lanthorn back and forth to spray light forward in the tall brush, but she was nowhere to be found. In the distance, he heard a shrill cry that made the hair on the back of his neck stand straight on end.

'Il Drago," he repeated as he fell to the forest floor in terror, "Il Drago."

He stroked her cheek and ran his adolescent fingers through the mane of long hair that rested in his lap. She had plainly exhausted all of her resources. Thank God they made it to the tree in time. Outside their makeshift shelter, Braeden could hear the wind whistling through the trees and the sounds of the forest creatures settling in for the night. An occasional howl reminded him to be ever on the watch. But it wasn't the wolves that frightened him most. It wasn't even the legendary dearg-due, the beautiful night creatures that would drain you of your blood before you could raise your broadsword. No. It was the thought that what he had done had been successful.

Had he managed to summon an actual dragon? Was that even possible? Would it serve him because he called it or would it kill him as soon as look at him? Would they ever be safe again and had he put the one person on this earth that he loved the most in danger? Would Orla ever be safe again?

He was tired of the battle that waged between the O'Malley and Burke clans. He was tired of hearing about it, tired of fearing for it and tired of preparing for it. It needed to end, for good, and soon. Hopefully a handful of dragons, under his command, could end it once and for all. At least that had been his plan. Now that he thought about it, how on earth would anyone control a dragon? Had he literally unleashed hell on earth? Would Patrick and Darina find it in their hearts to forgive him? Or would they fall victim to his latest adolescent whim?

Braeden knew that in just a few short summers, he would take up the mantle of Lord of the O'Malley clan. This was his rightful place, being the eldest son of the late Lord and younger brother to Darina. He just wanted to make sure when he sat in that position, there was no more Easal McCallister to worry about. He needed to make sure there was no witch - Odetta Burke - posing problems with her plotting and scheming. He needed to make certain that Orla would finally agree to be his, body and soul, and sit next to him in the council chamber, as his wife.

She stirred, ever so softly for a brief moment in his lap. A quiet little moan that reminded him he was all male slipped from her lips before she let out a deep sigh and surrendered to a shallow sleep. How long would he have to wait to make her his?

six

O'Malley Territory
Council Chambers

Riann?" gasped Darina. She rose from her seat next to Patrick and stared directly in front of her, towards the dead center of the council chamber table where a peregrine falcon closely resembling her own, Riann, sat perfectly still. Fanai, her hound, growled and picked up his ears in confusion.

The Falcon didn't move. Sitting motionless on the table, it stared intently back into the terrified eyes of Darina O'Malley. "Riann?" she questioned again, searching the faces of those with her in the chamber for some sort of explanation.

"Darina," spoke Airard softly. "This is not Riann. This is Gemma."

"Gemma?" gasped Darina covering her mouth in disbelief. There were Gemma's clothes lying in a puddle on the floor next to her seat at the table, there was a terrible noise and a flash of bright light and then suddenly, there was this falcon. It looked just like Riann. But that couldn't be, Riann was in her quarters, next to the stables where she was cared for until Darina would hunt, or practice, until she called for her. *Her* Riann.

"By the gods," Galen spoke out loud, unintentionally.

"What is the meaning of this?" her uncle Ruarc interjected, pounding his fist on the table, and frightening the falcon, Gemma, in the process.

"Calm down," Flynn interrupted. "Everyone just calm down a bit. There is a perfectly good explanation for this. And I for one am ready to hear it."

"Gemma," Patrick spoke up. "Mayhap you would like to explain this a bit," he nodded toward the bird, who appeared to nod in return. "Galen can you assist her behind the column please," Patrick gestured towards her clothes and the four foot diameter column on the north side of the council chamber.

"Aye, my Lord."

It only took a few moments before Gemma returned to the table, fully clothed and wearing her human form. She filled her goblet with wine and sat down slowly, the weight of what she was about to say consuming her face.

"I am a shifter," she sighed as a large tear slid down her cheek. "I have been a shifter since I was a wee child. I realized I was a shifter when me family and I were traveling through Burke lands to here. I was able to take the form of a rabbit when the rest of me caravan was taken as slaves to the piers, the shipyards." Her hands began to tremble. "I did what me grand mam told me, she said, "Gemma, ye pretend really hard to be someone else, something else and ye just may be able to escape."

"So I pretended I was a wee rabbit skipping and jumping through the brush, under the noonday sun. I heard the others screaming, but I just kept jumping and running. Soon I didn't hear them as much any longer. I imagined that I had perhaps fainted or passed out, but that wasn't so. Later, I woke up surrounded by soft fur and warmth in an underground tunnel. I was in a rabbit hole! I must have spent a good day with the rabbits before I realized I needed to figure out how get back to being me, again."

The tears were flowing freely now and Gemma wiped her face with the edge of her tunic.

"Go on, " Darina bade her, curiosity written across her face. "Go on."

"Well," continued Gemma, seeking approval from the rest of the clan with a passing inquisitive glance. "Well, it took me awhile but I finally was able to shift back into my human form. There I was in the middle of god-knows-where, a little wee babe, dirty and naked and covered in mud."

"What happened?" asked Lucian.

"As I lay behind some brush," she stopped to wipe a tear away. "It was nearing dusk mind ye," she added, "I was a watchin' the road and a group of merry ladies made to pass by me bush so I began throwing stones into the way, to see if I could catch someone's, anyone's attention."

"And did ye?" asked Darina.

"Aye," I did. "Claira Stewart happened to me and seeing my condition, wrapped her overcloak about me and set me upon her shoulders. The ladies were making their way back to the Island, to the boats after having worked in the fields for the day."

"Claira is yer mother," Darina interjected.

"Aye - she became me mam," Gemma replied, nodding in agreement. "I've no good idea who I really am, I was but a lass of three years I believe at the time."

"Dear God, without a family and loose in the lands at three," interjected Ruarc.

Gemma took a long swig from her goblet before continuing. "Later, Claira asked how I managed to escape the slavers. I told her my name because I remember being called Gemma, and then I told her about becoming a rabbit. At first she laughed until I thought she would cry. I was quite sure she thought I was mad on top of dirty and naked, but it wasn't a laugh of disbelief, more of a laugh of joy."

"What do you mean?" Flynn asked.

"Well, the laugh you make when you find something altogether familiar and humorous at the same time, I suppose," Gemma replied. "Because no sooner had I peeked my head over the washtub she stuck me in that I looked down to see a white rabbit right where Claira had stood just moments before."

"Claira was a shifter too?" Airard asked.

"Aye."

"What has any of this got to do with my Daenal?" interrupted Jamie Burke. "Time is a wasting and I've got to be moving along," he spoke sternly as he rose from his seat and alerted his guards to be ready to move.

"Wait, Jamie," Gemma replied. "Please wait a moment. I can help, I can go to Dragon's Point. None of you here can climb the face of that rock without getting killed, and ye know this. Ye'll either drown in the falls or fall and break yer necks. I can get there, I can get right into the lair and see if Daenal is there, and if she is, I can help you figure out how to get her out. Let me be the eyes and ears here. Let me, I know I can do this."

"And what if ye fail, Gemma?" asked Jamie. "What if the dragon eats ye afore ye can get back to us? What then?"

"Well, Jamie, I know that's possible. And I am willing to accept the risk. I love Daenal, I wouldn't dream of doing nothing here. Give me until sundown tomorrow. If I have not returned, then ye can count me as gone and ye all can make another plan, determine some other path for her rescue. Just please, at least let me try, for Daenal's sake."

"I just canna believe this is happening. A witch, a demon, a dragon, a shifter, by the god's what else will we encounter?" moaned Darina, as she rubbed her swollen belly. "I just don't know what to think ana'more, I really don't."

"Darina," said Patrick, "Gemma is our best hope. Let her go take a look at what is really going on here. Let her see if Daenal is really there if the dragon is in its lair at all, if she is alive. And if she is, we will see what can be done."

"Gemma, will ye take Fanai with ye?" Darina asked, motioning to her falconry hound lying next to her on the floor. "If something were to become of ye, if ye were to need some kind of assistance, Fanai will return and tell me."

"Don't ye look at me that way," Darina spat at a very hesitant Patrick. "This dog tells me all kinds of things, whether ye, believe it or not. It won't hurt nothing for him to go as far as he can see her and wait. If I tell him that is what he is to do, that is what he will do, I tell ye."

"Aye, Darina, I will take Fanai with me."

He sat quietly for a moment, gazing intently between the crackling fire on the hearth and the woman standing before him motionless. It was some time before he spoke, long moments that tried her patience and caused her to wrestle intently with her hands. Her hands were now clasped crudely in front of her as if they would escape were they given the chance. Her aura had changed since he last "saw" her. No longer a dark charcoal gray, it gave off the illusion of – could it be – happiness? Not sure what to do with that information, Jamie Burke sighed and tugged at his beard clasping his own hands in his lap.

The Burke refugee camp had become a quasi-independent village within the O'Malley territory. For the most part, Jamie was left to independently oversee the Burke clans people with only minimal involvement of the O'Malley Lord, Patrick MacCahan-O'Malley. It was. Nevertheless, Jamie Burke's duty to hear all manners brought before him, by a Burkes-man, even if the petitioner was his own mother.

The silence grew thick. He knew she would never speak first, and for a slip of time he reveled in the power he held over this woman. It was easy to hate her and pity her all at the same time. It was not her fault he had been taken from her at birth and sent off to foster elsewhere. Her father was a monster in his own right, and she had followed suit by practicing the black arts and making herself an enemy of their gracious hosts, the O'Malleys. Her story, though, if true, was fantastical. There was some otherworldly creature holding her hostage and forcing her to perform all manner of cruelty over her own people. All of this was in an effort to find some ancient relic. A relic that would somehow return him, her ex-husband, Easal, who used to be Eaton, to whatever black hole in the universe from which he had come.

He shook his head. It was too maddening to believe. But – the priest bought the story and sold it to Patrick as well. He sold it to the others, including Lucian, the clan scribe and druid priest, and his brother, Airard, from Patrick's clan in the north, and even the lad, Braeden, rightful heir to the O'Malley lordship. They all believed her, but seeing was not believing for Jamie. Having been blind from birth, he saw people and things in different ways than the others, and he hadn't yet made up his mind.

Yes, her aura had changed. Either she was making real, significant progress or she had harnessed the power of her black arts to the point she was able to fool even him. He knew about her and Kurt, the former priest although he doubted anyone else knew yet. He saw it in both of them whenever they were within ten feet of one another. They were drawn to each other like magnets like there was some invisible force bringing them to each other. He wondered if she had cast a spell or if their attraction spanned more than recent history. She had imprisoned the priest before, when she held the power in Burke lands. Back when Easal was still Easal, the captain of the Burke guards and Odetta's betrothed. Not the empty shell of a person now possessed by Eaton, the evil, manipulative, monster she claimed he now was.

"Well, let's have it then," he grumbled.

"My Lord," she began.

"Jamie, ye may call me Jamie," he curtly replied.

"Jamie," she sighed in relief, "please call me mam," she attempted to say sweetly, but the concept was clearly lost on her. She struggled with her hands before her in such a way as to lose her balance, and nearly tip herself over.

"Don't hurt yerself," he stated, smugly. "Odetta will suffice."

She nodded in submission, curtsied and stood upright, looking deep into his crystalline eyes, wondering what he really saw. Her aura changed to fear and hesitation and Jamie interjected.

"No reason for fear, Odetta, ye've made it thus far. What is yer request?"

"Well, Jamie, 'tis not so much a request as it is – advice."

"Advice? For me?" he chuckled.

"Aye."

This piqued his interest. "Please, sit ye there," he said motioning to a stool across from him at the table. "Please, do tell what advice ye have for me, milady."

"Well, as ye well know, Easal will not rest until the Island of Women is his and he has invaded and overtaken the O'Malleys, with our people here as well."

"I've heard tell," he nodded.

"Well, I have a way to defeat him. I have knowledge of certain – uh – circumstances that will come upon us and I believe it may be the way – the only way – we can defeat him."

"We?" he asked, "are ye considering yerself a "we" of the Burkes or a "we" of the O'Malleys?" he added sarcastically.

"Aye, we of this table," she responded, just as sarcastically. "As yer – uh – family, I care about what happens to ye as well as our people, whether they care for me or not. I've got just as much stake in the outcome and overtaking of Easal as ye do. Just as much," she added, between gasps, "and I'll not see ye stricken down in battle if it can be avoided."

"I don't see how war can be avoided, Odetta, if Easal intends to strike."

"I know you would see it that way, but that's why I must tell ye what I know. Ye must know and then ye can decide for yerself how best to move forward."

"Verra well then," Jamie signed loudly, "what is it ye think ye know?"

"I have a certain aptitude, well – knowledge, rather, that may assist us in the timing of a strike. Ye see, Jamie, I'm a star gazer."

"By the gods, woman, ye mean to distract me with yer black magic?" Jamie thundered as he rose from his seat. "I won't have any more of this nonsense...."

"Milord," a deep male voice echoed behind him. "Milord, I believe ye may wish to hear what Odetta has to say."

"Airard," Jamie replied softly to the elderly druid priest laying on a makeshift cot in the back of the great hall. "Airard, what knowledge have ye of star-gazing?"

"Verra little, I must confess," Airard continued, "However, I do know that it has nothing at all do with magic. I realize this may be a foreign concept to ye, lad, but as of yesterday, so were dragons, I hear."

"True," responded Jamie. "Verra well, please continue," he said, nodding towards Odetta.

"Milord," she began.

"Jamie, he replied sternly.

"Jamie," she said, "I have studied the charts for years, since I was but a youth," she twisted her hands tightly until they turned white. "I had many learned scholars give me instruction, and I can tell you that an event is coming which could make all the difference in the world to us as far as strategy."

"And pray tell how would star-gazing make any difference in the world?" he responded sarcastically.

"Jamie," gasped Airard in frustration, "please won't ye let her finish?"

"Aye, I will let her speak."

"Jamie, on a certain day, a fort-night and three nights from this verra day, the Sun will be hidden by the moon and make the daylight into total darkness for a few short minutes."

"An eclipse?" gasped Airard, "Aye – an eclipse, Jamie, don't ye see?"

"See what?" Jamie asked. "What has this to do with war?"

"Jamie," Odetta continued. "An eclipse during the daylight hours which turns the light into total darkness is the perfect way to ambush Easal and his men."

"Darkness?" Jamie asked. "Complete darkness? I've done raids afore at night and ye are not at such an advantage as one may think."

"But Jamie," continued Airard, "During the middle of the day, when they are not expecting darkness, the enemy would be powerless against us."

"Are ye sure about this Odetta?" Jamie asked.

"Aye, I know the day, hour, to the minute, to the second even," she responded.

"And ye trust her Airard?"

"Aye," replied the druid priest.

"How will I explain this to our men, how will I train them for such an attack?" Jamie asked.

"Who better to prepare the men to fight in darkness, Jamie?" Odetta said. "Ye, who have been in darkness since birth, ye, who has been in darkness for this verra purpose, ye will lead our people through the darkness and into daylight and victory!"

"Aye," replied Airard. "May it be so!"

seven

Burke Territory

easal scratched at his short beard and paced the perimeter of his darkened chamber. A chambermaid scrambled to make a fire in the hearth before encountering his wrath and unleashing a diatribe of indecipherable words as was his typical bed-time form. She wasn't sure what language it was that he spoke when he spoke thus, but she was sure she didn't want to be on the receiving end of it, whatever it was. Light from the hearth illuminated his chamber and cast foreboding shadows upon the wall. His shadow form was freakishly large, larger than any human she had ever seen and shaped much differently than that of a man. She knew Easal was a monster, she just didn't know he was really a monster, until now.

Sputtering out of the room backward, she made her obligatory bows first to Easal, then to Ochnar, his guard and lastly to Marina, his personal aide, and advisor. The woman gave her pause, sending chills up and down her spine. She wasn't sure who to fear more, Easal or Marina.

"Shall I find a replacement for *her?*" asked Marina to Easal sarcastically. "Ye've only gone through five maids in the last few weeks, what's another one?"

"Nay," retorted Easal, who sounded more tired by the moment. "I tire of learning their names. I haven't the patience to deal with it at the moment."

"Well, I'm certainly no' about to start cleaning yer chamber pot and bathing ye my Lord," she said. "I've more to offer than simple, domestic services," said the gray-haired Marina. She she ran her bony fingers along the outer edge of a pile of scrolls haphazardly strewn across the side table. "In fact, me thinks the services ye do require are those of a much, much younger lass. We both ken ye need a babe to take yer - uh - place in this world, and a younger lass can be both a companion and a maither for yer bairn."

"There are no 'lasses' to be found who would agree to such an arrangement, Marina."

"Aye, I must agree with you there. I think if ye went searching and found a lass that mayhap wasn't from around here, mayhap she might be amenable to such an arrangement, seeing as how ye are the Lord and all. There must be some match of sorts we can make with a lass from somewhere else, someone who hasn't heard all the rumors, perhaps someone who ye could mold into what it is ye need. Obviously, she should be someone willing to accept yer particular set of *proclivities* - yer circumstances. Someone who wouldn't care about the details. Someone who sees the power in the position of Lord's wife and who would be hungry to share just a little bit of that power." She set down the scroll she was holding and walked towards him, lightly stroking the edge of his cheek with the back of her hand.

"Easal, ye know there is more power in two than there is in jest one."

"I am not "jest one,'" the low sounding growl rolled off of his tongue and echoed throughout the chamber. It echoed against the walls, shaking the table and sending the logs in the fire crashing upon one another spewing ashes and light.

"Aye, aye, my Lord," she gulped in fear. "Of course, ye are more than jest one," she added. "But, the people, the clansman, they have fled our lands."

"Good riddance," he barked back.

"My Lord," she responded gently patting him on the shoulder, "Whether ye believe it or not, to get what ye need, ye need the Burke people themselves."

"What I need is to leave this place, as soon as possible!"

"I ken that is what ye want. I really do. But I also know that if the people believe that the lands – their lands – will be returned to them, they will return, and they will work for ye, for us, for their lands, their heritage, their families. Ye jest need to make them believe in ye that ye are on their side, that ye want them to belong here and that ye are not the monster that Odetta says that ye are. Make them truly believe that ye are Easal and they will come back home."

"Why would it matter to me if they were here or there? All I need is the nexus, it will get me home and I will never have to see these people ever again."

"Easal, don't ye see if the people believe in ye again, if they believe in the Burke clan, then they will help ye find whatever ye want. They will help ye take back the Island territory, they will do it for ye – their leader. They won't even need to know why they are doing it. By the time ye are gone, it won't even matter to them."

"Ugg," was the only reply that came from the large man who stood gazing out over the hills towards the sea. He was a mighty sight, large by anyone's standards, with long red-brown, flowing wavy hair that hung down passed his tartan, nearly touching his waist. His plaid was crinkled from his day's activities, but he wore it, it seemed to make the soldiers happy. His boots were mud-caked and worn and there was the slightest smell of sulfur that lingered. He'd been in the catacombs and Marina wasn't sure she wanted to know why.

"I'm no' altogether certain we've even the slightest possibility of finding a lass as ye describe. "Even if'n I subscribed to yer - uh - theory."

A low grunt interrupted their conversation. "Uh, my Lord, ye see," interjected the guard, "I believe I may know of someone who might fit that description," said Ochnar.

"Ye do? Do ye?" asked Marina. "Do tell then."

Easal grunted in return and nodded his head as he sat down with a thud against the back of the bench-once-a-church-pew along the far wall under the window, sending the bench scraping against the stone surface. "Go on with ye," he muttered.

"Well, sir, ye see, sir there are the prisoners."

"The prisoners?" asked Marina. "Why would we even consider a 'prisoner'" for such a station? Easal, we have prisoners? I thought all the prisoners had escaped with the refugees?"

"The ones from the shipwreck?" Easal asked, completely ignoring Marina's interjection.

Ochnar responded, "Aye, my Lord. As ye may recall, there were four survivors. They've been holding up in the Ole' Missus Edwards' cottage. Not prisoners per se' mind ye," he directed to Marina in particular. "But not free to go jest yet either."

"What have they to do with this Ochnar? Get to the point - quickly," Easal demanded.

"Well, my Lord, if memory serves me correctly and from what I can relay from the Ole' Missus, one of the survivors was a young lady. She is a might striking little lass when I think about it. Well, they were all discussing where they needed to be and where it is they were a'going after they were all well enough to get on by themselves. That lil' lass there said she had no idea where she would be a'going. That's on account of her fellow she was going to meet and marry in O'Malley Lands had gone and got himself entangled with one of the O'Malley sisters."

"An O'Malley sister?" Marina asked. "I wonder which one?"

"Well, and she only did know this on account of Naelyn, mind ye. Naelyn's sister Gemma told her when she went on that visit ye let her take, and then Naelyn told me and the Ole' Missus when we visited with the shipwreck survivors. Well, it seems that Flynn - that is the name of the fellow that she was a gonna marry..."

"Flynn?" shouted Easal. "Did ye say, Flynn?" he repeated banging his oversized hand on the bench beside him and rising at the same time.

"Aye, my Lord, a fellow by the name of Flynn Montgomery."

"Ochnar," whispered Marina, "That is the captain of the guards of the O'Malley clan! Ye mean all this time we've had the wife to be of the O'Malley clan, right her under our noses?"

"Well, I suppose I simply didn't know who this Flynn fellow is my Lord. My apologies, I assure ye had I known he was someone of such station, I would have told ye immediately."

"Who else knows?" asked Easal.

"What does she look like Ochnar?" Marina interrupted.

"Who else knows?" Easal shouted this time to Ochnar.

"Well, jest me and the Missus I suppose my Lord."

"Good, keep it that way, Ochnar. No one is to know she has any ties whatsoever to the O'Malleys. Is that clear? No one else, anyway," he added.

"What sort of lass is she?" asked Marina.

"Well," Easal spurted, "tell her."

"Well, she is verra pleasant to look at, I'd have to say that. She has long flowing golden hair, she's a might petite, pretty puckered lips and nice eyes. She's got herself a fiery temper though; she is downright murderous with rage over her beloved - I mean - her betrothed's dalliance. Seems she was dead set on being married to a man of high station and said something about 'cutting him down' for what he'd done. Sharp tongue too – whoo whee – that lass there has flowery speech if I ever did hear any," he laughed.

"I bet," Marina chuckled, "She's no doubt a full-fledged Scottish lass."

"Go on," Easal continued.

"Well, seems to me, my Lord, she is the type that might get really excited about the prospect of finer things, and being the Lord's wife," he said. "Jest from looking a' her ye can tell she has certain expectations, ye know, fine clothing and what-not. She would definitely look the part and she seems smart enough. I don't think she'd take too well to a philandering man though, from what the men accompanying her have said, she's pretty adept with a dagger," he chuckled, scratching his chin.

Marina chuckled, "I don't think we'd have to worry about that Ochnar, Easal is a mon of honor." She exchanged knowing glances with Easal and a plan was born. "Ochnar, please tell the Missus that the Lord requests the honor of her presence and that of the prisoners – our guests – please Ochnar, call them our "guests", tomorrow evening in the great hall. We will discuss their safe return to their ports of origin."

"Ye mean to send her back, do ye?" Ochnar asked, looking puzzled.

"Jest ye let me handle that part," said Marina. "Ochnar, I will have a missive for ye to deliver to the Missus, come back at sun-up for it, it will be ready then."

"Aye," he said as he bowed and backed his way out of the chamber, clear that he had been dismissed.

"Wait," grunted Easal. "What is this lass called?"

"Ah – I believe they call her Aisling."

eight

Dragon's Point

She watched as the red dragon tenderly groomed the young, blue, dragon, careful not to be rough with its malformed wing. She determined this must be the mother, and the young its offspring. No longer in fear for her life, *why else would she still be alive*, Daenal sat down peacefully against the stony wall and let the sounds of the water fall calm her into a peaceful oblivion. Of course, she still wondered why she was there, but realized that no amount of anxious imaginations would give her that answer, and so, she simply trusted. She trusted that she was here for a reason that she was needed, perhaps she could help and when the time came, she would be willing and ready to do so.

The young blue dragon knew she was there, having looked her in the eye several times, appearing to be just as inquisitive about her as she was of he. It was a "he" alright; the tell-tale signs of newly cut horns blistered the top side of its dark blue head. They had just finished their meal of fish and other sea creatures and curled up tenderly next to one another, grooming and preparing for slumber. She presumed as it was nearly sun up. The hare was putting off an inviting aroma after the red dragon tossed it upon a stone and lit it afire. Was it a *peace* offering of some kind? Daenal was growing very hungry and her low blood sugar told her to eat or sleep or pass out. She wasn't sure which would happen first, but she was ready to find out just how done the hare was at this point.

Reaching in her left boot, she retrieved the dagger her Uncle Ruarc gave her as a child and inched slowly on all fours towards the center of the cave, towards the stone containing Red's burnt offering. The dragons looked up only long enough to notice her movement and then turned away, back towards each other, to their bonding moment. It was surreal almost how caring they seemed to be with one another. *It's too easy to believe that unusual creatures are monsters, I suppose,* she thought to herself.

Tearing into the nearly well-done hare, Daenal ate her full. Never had she been more grateful for freshly cooked meat, seasonless or not. The young, blue dragon watched her, almost as if he were mesmerized by her skillful method of skinning, then fileting the already cooked gift from his mother. She had no doubt she was the first human form to have reached his eyes, and wondered secretly what they told each other when they looked at one another.

A flash of light caught her off guard and sent her reeling backward, towards the rocky cave wall behind her. Grasping her pounding head, Daenal rocked back and forth; hoping to stave off what she thought might be an impending migraine. The ground spun beneath her and almost as if she had fallen dead asleep, she was suddenly in a dream-like world. She was spinning, swimming and floating weightlessly above the cave floor, looking down upon her surroundings. Another flash and she was now on a rocky shoreline, watching from a distance behind rocks as five burly men struggled against something trapped in the dark. It was caught in a net, and it was fierce, angry, terrified and monstrous.

It let out a muffled shriek that struck her to her bones. With one loud thud, the largest man struck it about the head with his club and it fell to the earth in a crumpled mess, knocked clean out. It took all five men what seemed hours to load the tangled mess upon a flat wagon pulled by four horses. Light from the moon reflected off of the shore line and Daenal could see it was another dragon. A large male dragon with curled horns and a wingspan she dared not think about. Its snout was bound up so that it couldn't breathe fire and it was, therefore, at a severe disadvantage. How in the world had it managed to get itself caught by mere soldiers she wondered?

And then she saw them. There they were, the two smaller dragons hiding in the brush, not far off, watching as their champion was being carted off. He must have been protecting his family, the larger one. The King Dragon, they had captured a King Dragon! And now, his Queen and his progeny were alone, hiding in a cave atop the falls.

Is that how the blue dragon was wounded? Had they come to Daenal for help with the wound, or for help freeing their King? Daenal awoke from her haze and stood upright. Still dizzy, she made her way back towards the fiery stone where the remnants of the hare lay, and she stood there still staring into the solemn, molten eyes of Red, the Queen Dragon. For long moments they gazed at one another, she, a mere mortal, and she, a mere creature and they felt for one another. They were both apart from their loves, in unfamiliar territory, with nowhere to go. And they just stared, knowingly.

He was kicking again, and he was serious about something. Darina knew he was a boy, but couldn't quite explain to anyone just how she knew. Of course, she was frightened to say as much, especially to her husband, Patrick. He already thought she was daft, and they were having issues of their own already.

The noon day sun was high in the sky and cast a bright glow across Darina's rosy face. Shielding her eyes with her hands, Darina moaned as the cold white hands pressed hard against her stomach. Vynae pulled Darina's thin linen shift back down over her swollen belly and sighed. The elder healer was concerned about the pregnancy and wasn't tactful about it either.

"Darina," she sighed, "Eets gonna be a large one," Vynae breathed heavily. "I can't see how ye have much longer, although by yer own calculations ye be a claiming another fortnight."

"Aye," Darina signed, patting her belly as she rose from the sturdy wooden bench. Straightening her over robe as she stood, she grasped the edge of the bench with her left hand when she stumbled forward. She was *ripe*, like her sister Dervilla would say, and it was getting harder just to breathe, let alone stand up.

"Well, ye know," continued Vynae, "I can make ye a brew that will bring it on sooner, and save ye the struggle, lass. That one there, she pointed with her bony index finger, is gonna be like passing a camel through the eye of a needle, she half-laughed, half-warned.

Darina grimaced and fiddled with the torque around her neck, stroking it for good luck as she remembered her cousin Kyra's difficult delivery. The twins had been hard on Kyra, but Kyra was a strong one and the twins were healthy, after all. That was really all Darina needed to know.

"Yes, I think he is gonna be large, like Patrick," Darina agreed.

"He?" chuckled Vynae. "Ye think it's a boy, even after all these years with the Burke curse? Darina, ye know a male child hasn't been born to an O'Malley family in many, many years. Odetta Burke saw to that, milady."

"Except for me brathair Braeden, remember?" Darina interjected sarcastically.

"Aye, yes, except for Braeden," Vynae agreed.

"And – Aiden," she added, referring to Kyra's twin son.

"Aye, that's right milady," Vynae agreed, "But those bairns were conceived elsewhere Darina. Yer brathair was conceived in Scotland and Aiden most likely was conceived in Burke lands."

"Aye, and Patrick and I have been elsewhere as well," Darina added, glaring purposefully at the nosey woman, "'Tis not like we haven't stepped outside our territory ever, Vynae. Besides, Odetta is in our charge now, any curse that may have been, having long since been broken, I'd say, wouldn't ye?"

"Well, I guess I wouldn't know," Vynae added feigning disinterest. "I should like to see ye, every other day now, for at least the next six days, more as it gets closer. I'm thinking as big as this 'boy' is - ye waters will break first and then we'll be in the thick of it. Does Patrick plan on being with ye?" she asked hesitantly. "Ye young ones, ye do it different than I'm accustomed."

"Of course, he does," spat Darina, "He was there for the conception; he'll be there for the birth. He was there with me cousin Kyra, why wouldn't he be for me?"

"Well, I didn't rightly know that, seeing as how I wasn't there for Kyra's delivery."

"I'm sorry, Vynae," she said, "I forgot ye were asked to leave. It was a difficult birth and Parkin was terrified, I can't think of any other reason you wouldna' be welcome to attend to the matter. Patrick's brathairs, well all of them, the whole lot of them MacCahan boys, they are stubborn as wild mules. Ye will most definitely attend to mine, will ye no' though?"

"Of course I will Darina, I attended ye own birth meself. I wouldna' think of leaving ye to anyone else."

The sound of pounding footsteps down the hallway broke the conversation and Kyra burst into the chamber. "Darina, ye must come at once, at once."

"What is it Kyra," Darina asked, looking puzzled as her face switched between Kyra and then back to Vynae.

"'Tis Fanai" Kyra gasped, "He hasno' returned? Yer hound, he hasno' returned and Jamie has called a council meetin'. Parkin is gathering his men from the ship and they are all set to leave, Patrick needs ye at once."

"Aye," Darina replied, "I'm close behind."

nine

Burke Lands

The trio was nearly exhausted, having run, walked, trudged and dragged themselves through the forest for the past five hours. They had still not reached the border between O'Malley lands and Burke lands and now their hunger was getting the better of them. The two lasses sat down beside a babbling brook, intent on resting, regardless of what their slave-driver for a self-appointed leader had to say about it. Splashing water all over her face, Naelyn lay back down against the low brush and soaked up the sun.

"We *must* be getting on," Braeden said for what seemed the hundredth time in the previous ten minutes.

"I don't rightly care what ye think about it ana'more," Orla quipped, "We need to rest and eat something, Ana'thing – and there is no way ye can be a 'carrying the both of us. Especially since ye carried her for miles already," she said nodding at Naelyn.

"How did ye happen upon me ana'how?" asked Naelyn to Braeden.

"Well, I was gathering some wood for a fire and I heard yer voices, talking real low like and I watched as the lanthorn went out. So, I jest sat there behind a bush and waited to see what would happen. It appeared ye might need some help so I waited and watched and when the moment was right, I grabbed ye."

"Why on earth would ye help me Braeden, after all I did to ye? After putting ye in the dungeon, and nearly sacrificing ye with Odetta in the ceremony and all? I figured ye might wish to kill me instead. I certainly would," Naelyn whispered. It had only been a few months since their last meeting and it still weighed heavily in Naelyn's mind. All the things she had done for, with and on behalf of Odetta Burke. But that was then and this was now, and Braeden had just helped her escape the Roman soldier and her eventual placement in the catacombs with that *thing*. She couldn't even imagine it and wondered if Braeden had heard everything that had been said.

"Well," said Braeden, rubbing at his chin and tugging on his day's old stubble, "I had that thought, but then I remembered all the good things that Orla said about ye, during the council meetings and the investigations and such. I figured ye may be put to good use somehow."

"Orla said good things about me?" Naelyn asked, surprised.

"Aye, she did," returned Braeden, nodding his head and chuckling at the sound of Orla's snoring. "Said ye were much like a second mathair to her, and that means something, especially for Orla; who hasn't had much of a mam at all."

"Well, I'm glad to hear that Braeden, I really do care for her."

"But ye know what I really want to know about don't ye?" he asked.

"What do ye mean?"

"Ye know, I want to hear about *eldrago*," he said with inflection, making a point.

"I was afraid ye heard," Naelyn sighed. "I don't know much about dragons Braeden, only what I've read, which is probably jest the same stories that ye have read. Mostly fables and fairy tales, really, I'd know idea they actually existed."

"Why was the solider taking ye with him then if ye don't know ana'thing about 'em?"

"That's the thing Braeden, I don't rightly know. I guess Easal thinks I may be able to do something with a wild creature that he can't. He has it locked down in the catacombs. I'm afraid to think what might happen if they don't let it loose soon."

Orla shot straight up from her half-slumber on the bank of the brook. Scratching at her disheveled hair, she turned to face Braeden, "Braeden, ye mean to say that it worked?"

"What?" he asked.

"The summoning - ye mean to say ye actually summoned a dragon and Easal has it in the catacombs?" Orla asked.

"Ye summoned the dragon?" Naelyn gasped, pointing absent-mindedly at her adolescent savior. "Braeden what have done? How on earth did you summon a dragon? Oh! By the gods! Ye have awakened a dragon! Do you know? Is it a King Dragon? Oh, by the gods, Braeden! What have you done?" she shook her head and began pacing back and forth in front of the bubbling water, nearly tripping over Orla in the process.

"How am I to know what manner of dragon they have caught? I haven't seen it - and if I had, I don't know that I would know what kind it is," said Braeden. "I'm not a dragon master."

"What's a king dragon, Naelyn?" Orla interrupted.

"We need to be going now," said Braeden motioning for them to follow. Pushing aside the high brush that just bordered the shoreline, he ventured into the sandy area a bit. Now that the sun was up, sentries wouldn't find it unusual for people to be in the area, and it was less likely they would be stopped or questioned. Traveling along the shoreline would make their journey easier and bring them close to some piers from which they could maybe do some fishing. "I think we can stop in an hour or so, and see what we might catch with this net I found."

"What's a King Dragon?" Orla repeated this time softly, to Naelyn.

"Shhh...," said Naelyn, waving at Orla, "Not now."

"They've been whispering like that for hours," Kurt offered smugly. "I can't say as how I ken anathing about what they do or do not know about dragons or anathing else for that matter," he shook his head in aggravation. "I get that they are both scribes, brothers and druid priests," he added, motioning towards the table where Airard and Lucian sat conversing quietly with Patrick. "But what in the world do ye 'spose it means to be a Dragonian?"

"I 'ave no idea meself," Tragus remarked slowly. "Never heard tell of it. Have ye?" he asked, grunting towards Flynn Montgomery, Chieftain of the O'Malley militia and Patrick's Scottish cousin.

"Aye," Flynn grunted back, keeping his eye steadily locked on Dervilla O'Malley, who was seated halfway across the great hall breaking fast with her sister.

"Well," quipped Kurt.

"Well," added Tragus.

"Well, what?" grunted Flynn.

"He's no' paying ana attention a' all to us," Kurt remarked, slapping his hand down on the hard wooden table in front of Flynn. "Are ye?" Kurt added.

Flynn jumped, spilling his mug all over the platters of pork in front of the men, and turning over his stool in the process, landing belly up against the hard stone floor. The great hall erupted in laughter and servants scurried about to clean up the mess. Kurt reached down an arm to help him up while Tragus straightened the stool for him, inviting him to give it another try.

"Ye sure have yer mind on other things, do you no'?" asked Tragus, slicing a knowing glance towards Dervilla and back again at Flynn.

"I suppose I do," Flynn admitted, straightening his tartan about his shoulders.

"They're talking about ye, milord," said the maidservant to Flynn, as she refilled his mug and set it back down next to his fresh platter. "Verra interesting conversation if ye ask me," she added coyly before turning towards Tragus' mug.

"What do ye mean?" chuckled Kurt, "They're talking about Flynn?"

"Aye," she replied, "About Flynn and he's betrothed, mind ye. 'Bout them both even."

"Aye, I ken what ye are a'saying," said Tragus."But Dervilla O'Malley, the Lord's sister-in-law, she is no' Flynn's betrothed," he remarked gesturing towards Dervilla's table.

"Do ye think me dense? Of course, everyone knows Dervilla O'Malley 'tis, not his betrothed. She has might near a year going on her military commission yet, she can't be getting a'married *and* serve in the militia."

"Flynn has no betrothed. What are ye talking about?" ask Kurt.

"I think they said the lass's name was Aisling or some other such something like that. Anahow, I've got to be serving some other tables. I suggest ye ask Flynn there for clarification," she added pointing at a pale white Flynn Montgomery. "If anyone should know about Flynn's betrothed it should be Flynn."

ten

Burke Lands

She sat in the corner on the wobbly stool provided by her host and peeled potatoes in silence. It was a chore she had only recently become accustomed to, and she dreaded it. She knew better than to complain, it wouldn't help anyway and at least she would be able to confirm that the food she would eat was clean. She was still sore from tossing and turning on the floor the night before, but she was feeling stronger every day. The abrasions on her face were nearly healed, thanks to the salve administered by the portly Missus Edwards. The black eye would most likely take a little longer. It didn't appear the scratches would leave a permanent mark and for that she was thankful. She had survived most of her life on her looks alone, and lately that was literally all she had left.

Reluctantly on her way to a foreign land, to marry a man she had come to resent, Aisling McTavish was now a picture of desperation. She hadn't made it to her destination in time to intercept the missive she sent. She regretted that. She regretted a lot of things. Mostly, she regretted that her station in life required that she "marry up" in order to have anything. The missive to Flynn would have long since arrived. The missive would tell him she did not love him, that she would not agree to be his wife and that she would never, ever, ever leave Skye or her people. He was a fool for expecting her to do so. Their engagement was off and she never wanted to hear from him, ever again.

It *would* tell him, more likely it already had. Before she had a chance to intercept it, before she could arrive at O'Malley port before the letter would arrive. She had constructed a scenario in her mind a thousand times and in a thousand different ways on why she sent it and why she came to marry him anyway. She would plead and beg forgiveness and hope beyond hope, he would have her because there certainly was nothing left for her anymore, not in Scotland.

She watched as Ochnar discussed what appeared to be something of great importance and, evidently, some secrecy with Missus Edwards. He nodded, she nodded, they patted each other on the shoulder. The Missus appeared to be making a list of things in her head, adding things up, measuring her skirt, and bending down under her cupboard to look for something. Something was going on and Aisling wasn't sure she wanted to know.

"Aisling, dear," said the Missus, "bring me that clay jar from above the hearth, there. Aye, that one right there, "she pointed.

Curious, Aisling rose from her perch and tiptoed to reach the green colored, clay jar sitting high atop the shelf just above the hearth. She handed it to the Missus and returned to her work in the corner, feigning disinterest.

"Now here, ye take this right here and ye get the cloth I spoke of, take it over to the seamstress's shop. They have her size on hand and tell them to add the gold stringers to it, ye hear?"

Ochnar mumbled something Aisling didn't understand and took off quickly out of the cottage.

"Aisling dear," called the Missus. "I have some verra exciting news for you, well for us, actually."

"Aye," she replied. "What news? Is it about me leaving?"

"Nay, nay, nothing of that sort. I think ye and I both know ye haven't a chance now of making a go in O'Malley lands. We haven't heard from em, and we're on the brink of war even, as I told ye. Me poor dear lass, I think ye know there lies a largely burned bridge between ye and yer Flynn. It's too late, me dear. If'n he had inkling to come for ye, I'm sure he would've afore now."

Aisling nodded her head in agreement. It was true, it was too late with Flynn and she wasn't really all *that* sorry. She *was* still angry, and she wouldn't be the reluctant wife of a man who took her from her country. She just wouldn't. By now, he'd received the letter and he was just as angry at her as she was at him, and that was that.

"Well, I can't see what kind of news ye could have for me which may be ana 'good', but do go on. Please," Aisling whispered. "What has Ochnar to do with it?"

"Aisling," continued the Missus, "We have been invited to dine with the Lord of Burke lands and his mini-council tomorrow eve. As a survivor of the ship wreck, he has waited to make introductions until now, until he thought ye might be feeling a wee bit more like yerself."

"Why would the Laird wish to meet *me*?" Aisling asked, puzzled.

"That's just it, my dear," sighed the Missus, "I'm not supposed to say this, Ochnar swore me to secrecy but *Lord* Easal is seeking a bride. Yer name came up in conversation and well now, he wishes to meet ye."

Aisling let out a long, expressive sigh and set down at the table, rubbing her throbbing head. "What sort of mon is this Laird McCallister?"

"What's wrong me dear? Are you no' wishing to meet the Lord?"

"Well, I guess I should, I've no other options afore me now do I?"

"Well, of course, ye do, dear. Yer a pretty lass and any mon would be fortunate to have ye to wife. Lord McCallister is an honorable mon, recently divorced ye know from that old witch, Odetta. Their union didn't last verra long, I can tell ye that. I hear tell he's mighty handsome as well though I've never seen him meself. And just think - ye'd be the Lord's wife. We call him 'Lord' here Aisling, not Laird like in Scotland. Anyhow, seems Ochnar put yer name in seeing as how ye've nowhere to go and ye'r a pretty lass, and a strong one. Ochnar thought ye might like to make his acquaintance."

"Thank you, I suppose I shouldn't miss the chance. I suppose I'll be living here in Burke lands anaway, might as well be at the castle keep," Aisling chuckled.

"What was it ye gave Ochnar?" she asked.

"I gave him some coin to have ye a fine dress made, dear lassie. Yer shift and tunic will no' do for the castle keep and ye can't wear anathing of mine. I saved a bit up and now ye shall have a fine dress."

"Missus Edwards," replied Aisling astonished, "Ye know I haven't the coin to repay ye. Ye shouldn't have done that," she shook her head, "Now what will I do?"

"Aisling dear, I'm no' worried a bit about the dress. Besides, if things work out betwixt ye and the Lord, I'll be set for life."

"Whatever do ye mean?" asked Aisling.

"Well dear, I'm yer sponsor. Seeing as how ye are here from a foreign land with no family to speak of, in my charge since ye arrived, I'd be receiving yer tribute."

"I have no tribute here to speak of. I'm afraid there wouldn't be anathing for ye."

"Oh no, that's not what Ochnar said. Ochnar said the Laird will be paying a hefty tribute to the family of the lass he chooses, with a second tribute after the first son is born."

"My. Oj my," gasped Aisling. "Really?"

"Oh yes, dear. And since ye haven't ana family, I'd be taken up residence alongside ye in the castle keep. Wouldn't that be fine, Aisling?"

"Fine indeed," responded Aisling, all too clear now why the Missus was sold on the idea.

eleven

O'Malley Lands

Patrick scratched the back of his neck in frustration. Sitting at his desk in the Lord's official chamber, he attempted once again to contact his beloved Darina with his mind. It was something that he had been able to do from the very moment they first met, some months ago, just prior to their arranged marriage.   He called to her telepathically but received neither a response nor was he able to detect her at all. Normally he would be able to somehow decipher her thoughts or emotions. This had happened at only one time prior and it had been because of her deliberate refusal to let him in.

He hadn't asked her about it yet. No, not since the trouble with her sister being carried off by the creature. He wasn't sure he really wanted to know if she was doing it on purpose or if he had simply lost touch with his young bride. His work had been daunting in his this new foreign place. He wasn't even sure if the clan approved of him, with all of the turmoil going on between them and the Burke clan. It was enough that he had welcomed the Burke refugees from the north, but since he also welcomed the Burke witch, he partly feared for his life. There were many who did not agree with that move, and he was ever vigilant for himself and his bride.

But now, he was late, very late as a matter of fact, for a special meeting called by Jamie who represented the Burke clan. Jamie asked he come at once, and Patrick wasn't usually inclined to run to just anyone seeking his audience. But this was Jamie, and seeing as how Jamie was blind, it was probably easier to go to him than vice versa.

"Ruarc," Patrick called down the hallway, "are ye ready to go?"

"Aye, my Lord," responded Ruarc.

"Well, let's be off then," said Patrick, placing the scrolls on his desk inside the large bottom shelf behind his desk.

"Milord," said Ruarc, "Master Jamie has requested we meet in the council chamber below ground, says it will prove more private."

Puzzled, Patrick nodded his head in agreement and followed Ruarc down the flights of stony stairs that finally led to the secret passageway beneath the great hall. "Is it to be just Jamie and I then, Ruarc?" he asked.

"Aye, I believe so milord."

"Nay," came a voice behind them as they cleared the passage door, "I'm coming as well, Jamie called for me too."

"Flynn," said Patrick, "Good to have ye with us. Have ye any idea what this is about?"

"Not a one," he said shaking his head.

Her head had stopped pounding, but her stomach was swimming. She hovered in and out of sleep for what seemed hours, only to begin *hallucinating*? There she was again, the annoying woman, shaking her by the shoulders and bidding her remain quiet at the same time. Shaking, shaking, shaking and shaking her some more. Daenal groaned and attempted to roll over. The hard stony ground of the cave was not a suitable bed, but it had to do since it was all she had.

"Daenal," said the familiar voice. "Daenal, wake up lass."

Daenal scratched at her head and tested her weary back, attempting to sit up against the cave wall. Perhaps that hare wasn't fully cooked, after all. Fearing she may throw up, she placed her hands on the floor beside her, but something blocked her attempt to rise.

"Daenal, wake up."

She was cold, for some reason. Her overcloak was gone, she was sure she had wrapped herself in it just before lying down. A cold, damp cave was no place for a girl wearing only a thin linen shift. At least her feet and legs were warm, protected by her wool stockings and boots. What had become of the overcloak? Certainly the creature would not have taken it?

Rubbing the sleep from her eyes, she pressed her spine backward against the stony wall, hoping to stretch the sore muscles. Hands grabbed her shoulders again and Daenal at once was fully awake.

"Gemma?" she inquired hesitantly.

"Hush, child, ye'll wake the dragons," replied Gemma, motioning with her head towards the bowels of the cave.

"Gemma, how?..." Daenal began, before noticing Gemma was wearing her missing overcloak and little else.

"There'll be no time for discussions Daenal, I'm here to check on ye and make sure ye are still alive. I see that ye are. Have ye been hurt lass?"

It took a moment for Daenal to register what exactly was happening. How Gemma had reached the mouth of the cave was beyond her imaginings. There were no scratches or tell-tale signs that Gemma had been brought here by Red, and she knew Gemma wouldn't possibly be able to climb the face of the rock.

"Nay, I'm no' hurt," she replied, attempting to stand.

"Nay, please, stay jest there," said Gemma. "I don't want to wake the creature. Tell me, do ye fear for your life?"

Daenal knew she really wasn't afraid for her life. She shook her head again. She knew she wasn't hurt and that she wasn't about to be hurt. She wasn't sure why she was there, but she knew there had to be a good reason.

"I...I...I'm fine, Gemma. What about Jamie, is Jamie....is he....is he gone Gemma?" A tear trickled down her cheek as she thought about the one person on the face of the earth that she loved more than herself. What had become of the man who had won her heart and her hand at the games? Would they ever see each other again?

"Jamie is fine, Daenal. He wasna' harmed at the games. He is worried about ye though. That's why I'm here. He intends to bring troops with him, up here - to get ye."

"Oh, Gemma, he can't do that," Daenal replied. "I don't know how Red will react. It's simply not safe. Please do turn him around, send him back, please."

"Red?" asked Gemma.

'Red," replied Daenal, motioning towards the snoring red dragon.

"Ah, I see," Gemma responded, half attempting a smile.

"Why are ye here, lass?" Gemma asked matter-of-factly. She straightened the overcloak about her bare form and shivered for a second, taking in her surroundings. It was cold, damp and harsh inside the cave. She could see the remnants of a half eaten hare just feet away and knew that Daenal had sustenance. Obviously the creature didn't mean her to starve to death. There was plenty of water, whether or not it was fresh or safe was another matter, but Daenal appeared to be in no acute distress.

"I believe I was brought here to help her somehow, or him."
"Him?"

"Aye, there is another here with us, a young male I believe, he appears to be wounded. Perhaps I a meant to assist in his healing or perhaps there is another reason."

"I see," Gemma said. "Daenal, I'm not sure if or how ye can, but if ye can communicate with Red, ye need to make sure she understands ye must be returned as soon as possible. I am not altogether certain what will happen if ye don't. And - if ye don't, I think a wounded little dragon will be the least of Red's worries. Jamie is quite beside himself."

"Gemma?" asked Daenal.

"Aye, Daenal?"

"There's more." Daenal stood against the cave wall, taking in her predicament. Should she tell her about the other Dragon, the King Dragon or should she take one problem at a time? She needed to get word back to her sister, Patrick, Jamie and the others that she was safe and alright for the moment, but they had to know about the King Dragon. Oh! What did it all mean?

"Gemma, there is another *him*."

"Another him?"

"Aye, there is a King Dragon. *Their* King Dragon," she said, motioning towards the sleeping creatures, "and from what I can tell, Easal has him in Burke lands."

twelve

O'Malley Lands
The Port – Commerce District

The elder merchant scratched figures on a parchment, dipped his quill in ink, struck through the figures and started his figuring all over again. Scratching his head, he glared at Dervilla O'Malley in astonishment.

"Ye actually mean to say ye need four hundred of these things in less than nine days?"

"Aye", replied Dervilla.

"Well, if'n ye weren't the Lord's own seesta, by marriage, of course," he began, tapping his chin, "I'd tell ye ye were a daft lassy."

"I am in no way daft, sir."

"Well, I guess, well, let's see what I can do for ye. And, it has to be nine days? Whatever on earth on ye going to do with all these fishing nets, ye intend to resell these somewhere else for a hefty profit lassy?"

"Nay. As I just stated, they are needed for a miliary matter of great importance," Dervilla interjected, handing him the commission log signed by Flynn. "We must have these, in nine days, the security of O'Malley lands is at stake."

"Well, I can't tell ye rightly that we can make all of these in nine days," he said, eyeing his large workshop, "but what we can't make, we can certainly purchase. I'll need some funds upfront of course."

"Of course," replied Dervilla, setting a heavy sack of coins down with a thud. "Will this help?"

He chuckled, opened the bag and peeked inside, "Indeed it will. Indeed, it will."

Opening the large workshop door, Dervilla O'Malley pondered her predicament. Commissioned for at least ten more months in the military, she was in no rush to leave her station, but she wasn't exactly happy to be trapped within it either. Falling in love with Patrick's cousin Flynn, who was captain of the military hadn't been her plan. She knew her brother-in-law wouldn't be happy about it either. She had really only agreed to her commission to avoid being the prize at the clan games. When her sister Daenal took her place, she was relieved, a feeling that fed her guilt on a near daily basis.

She knew that Flynn shared her feelings toward him, but that considering he was her commander, wouldn't give voice to them. It was an unspoken knowledge they held between one another. When word came that his betrothed, Aisling had changed her mind and was actually coming to their territory from Scotland, to wed Flynn, her heart was nearly torn to pieces. His face shared his disappointment as well. She wasn't sure she would make it through a wedding between the man she cared so much about and a woman who obviously did not share her same sense of respect, admiration and infatuation.

"A reluctant wife," Aisling's missive read. How shockingly cold and unfeeling the words were. How Dervilla ever thought she would manage to stay away from Flynn Montgomery was beyond her. Perhaps after her commission ended she would simply leave, marry off to another clan and save her poor heart the torment, and her body the temptation. As it stood, she was quite nearly giddy each time she saw him. They had only shared the one kiss, but there was so much fire and passion, she was certain the next time would burn them both.

Patrick's brother Parkin was the one who brought the news. The ship had been lost at sea. All that remained was some burnt debris. It was like the other lost ships, some how firebombed from god-knows-where? There were no survivors.

Flynn had asked for her several times since word came of the death of Aisling, but she refused his invitations. Of course, as it pertained to the military, she obeyed every order and followed every protocol. She was unclear if she could maintain any sense of decorum in his presence if not chaperoned. He was always kind with his eyes and seemed to understand her hesitance. Had it not been for her commission, she was certain she would have had him before now. He had been invited, of course, to the Island of Women for the Lunar Festival and she was certain to be there. But it was her sister, in the end, who put a stop to her plan, reminding her of her duties to the clan, proper behaviour befitting a Lord's daughter and the fact that he was her captain. In the end, Dervilla was not ready to give up her commission or bring shame upon her family and Flynn mysteriously became ill and did not attend.

Today was different. Flynn had called for her and for Bahri, Gemma's second in command from the Island. There was some speculation on her part, but she feared the coming war, and could assume only that Flynn's request accompanied a plan with regard to the Burke's invading the Island; something the women had feared for a long time.

Dervilla bent down to tie her bootstrap for the third time in as many hours. Her mind was elsewhere and she knew it, and he would know it if she didn't get it together, and fast. The mere thought of him made her blush. Her pulse raced and she became hot and tingly. If she didn't get this man off her mind and fast, she would be in trouble, deep, deep trouble. How could she function? How would she be equipped to do battle if her every thought were of her commander and the gloriously wicked things she wished he would do to her?

A strong hand reached down towards her and she grasped it. How had he found her?

"I came to meet ye," said Flynn. "Let me help ye up." His pale green eyes were swimming with passion and resolve and she gulped. The warmth from his touch sent shivers down her spine and her stomach leaped into her neck. *Let go of his hand.* She kept repeating it to herself over and over, but somehow she had still not broken contact. *Let go of his hand,* she repeated to herself, somehow still frozen. As if she were simply a spectator, she watched as the object of her desire raised her left hand to his sultry mouth and placed a tender kiss atop it.

"Dervilla," he whispered slowly against her wrist, "I've been calling for ye." He released her from his grip and stood magnificently still before her. He was a good head and shoulder's taller than she and at least ten years older, but he was no match for Dervilla. She owned him, body and soul, he just did not know it yet. And - he had come to give her the worst possible news. How would he ever live with himself knowing what he was about to tell her?

Aisling placed the finishing touches on her long blonde hair as the Missus tightened the straps on her dress one last time. Her boots were new, her dress was new, her hair was freshly washed and now keenly adorned with flowers. Aisling was pretty as a picture and ready for the next stage of her life. If all went as planned, by the new moon she would be the Laird's wife, move into Castle Burke and be well on her way to running the "kingdom" as it were. The Burke Clan itself, although in some disarray, would come to accept her. Yes, she was a Scot, but she was beautiful, intelligent and likable when she tried and she was certain she could make this remnant of a clan do her bidding, willingly.

There weren't many of the true Burke clan left, most having fled to O'Malley territory several months back, along with the witch Odetta Burke, her soon-to-be husband's ex-wife. Rumor had it that Easal was not acting as Easal at all, and he had intercepted power which did not belong to him by overthrowing the council and banishing his wife; both of which sent shivers of excitement through Aisling. *A mon after me own heart*, she thought to herself. There weren't many things that excited Aisling. A man not afraid to take what he wanted was one of them, however.

Having scratched, plotted, schemed, stolen, cheated and worse to get by in her short nineteen years, Aisling was on the precipice of an enormous opportunity she would not let go to waste. She would be the new Lord's wife and she would rule. There would be no doubt about that. She may not have had a lot of experience with men, in that way, but she knew how to get what she wanted and she knew how to concoct a brew that would control them or end them. Her daily walks were testament to her knowledge of the herbs and roots and this man, like every other, would cause her no grief. She would get what she wanted and maybe, just maybe, if he were nice, she would let him live.

It would take some time, but it wouldn't be long until she would be privy to the council scrolls and she would find out what would become of the Laird's wife in the event of his death. If it were anything like her own clan back home, she would remain in power until his son was old enough to take the reigns. A son she would bare him, but not for a long, long, long, long time.

She smiled a wicked, knowing smile into the looking glass before her, grasping tightly about the round glass container in her pocket. It held the key to her salvation, and to her final act of revenge on Flynn Montgomery. Soon they would be enemies, literally. Soon she would have her vengeance and he would know the power of her resolve once and for all.

thirteen

O'Malley Lands

Marina poured him another glass of wine and sat down quietly across from Easal. The Lord's chamber was not her favorite place to meet, but it would have to do. He had been feeling ill since early in the day, throwing up and running and fever - and all this gave Marina pause. Having consulted nearly every text she could find, she was sure she had no idea what to do or what to think about her supposed "immortal" Lord's health crisis.

"Milord," she began softly, wiping the sweat from his brown. "Are ye quite certain it was something ye ate?"

"Aye," he mumbled gruffly. "Aye, the venison, I'm sure of it."

"Well, do ye think ye'll be in any mood to entertain our guests this eve?" she asked shaking her head. Contemplating all the work that had gone into putting the dinner together and perhaps making a match with the young lass to wed the Laird, she was worried.

"Aye, the peppermint oil has helped." He sat up on the edge of the bed and dangled his weak feet towards the floor.

"Milord," Marina began.

"I ken what ye are about to say, I know ye have questions," he said, more softly than she ever believed he would. He appeared, at the moment, almost *human* somehow.

"Ye do?"

"Aye, I do." Rising to his feet, he ventured toward the pitcher and basin on his side table. Grabbing a thin linen cloth, he washed his face, neck and hands and proceeded to tie his lightly graying hair with a leather thong about the base of his neck. "I *am* immortal, Marina."

"But?" she questioned.

"But, this *body* is not," he said, patting his stomach for emphasis. "It is dying and I've need to find another. I've been here a verra, verra long time and if I canno' leave here soon, I will need to find another, more suitable shell."

"And, what happens, milord if..."

"Do no' ask that jest yet. I've no plans to face that scenario anatime soon."

He was a striking man, or he was, or he is, which she wasn't exactly sure. He wasn't really Easal, he was Eaton, a being from some other place or time and he had assumed Easal's body. She hadn't believed the rumors in the beginning herself, but she'd been with him long enough to know it was so. The elderly druid preistess was reluctant to serve him at the start, but what other choice did she really have? When Odetta fled to Burke lands leaving her and the others alone, she had run out of options.

Easal was kind but firm, he had certain expectations but he was fair and he was clear. He wasn't always forthcoming with information, but she suspected that was as much for her benefit as anything else.

"We haven't had many conversations about what would, what will happen, Marina."

"Aye, milord, I've tried to respect yer privacy. I knew that when ye were ready, ye'd tell me what ye felt important."

"Aye, Marina," he said, swishing his mouth with mint water, before spitting it back into the basin.

"Easal's body, it is, well...it is not well."

"I see."

"I think maybe, this body has a couple of years at the most. If I haven't found another, more suitable body by that time, well - that wouldn't be good."

She looked at him in astonishment, he wasn't saying he would die, but he wasn't saying he wouldn't either.

"Ye see, I must have a body in order to leave here. Becoming Easal was important because I am the Lord here. I can get things done, I can perhaps find the Nexus and make my way home. Without the Nexus, I can never leave, Marina."

"What happens if ye do not find a body Easal?"

"It is much easier for me to assimilate into a body from a body, than without it. It's very complicated and difficult and will set me back hundreds, possibly thousands of years."

"Why a bairn Easal, why would you want an infant?"

"Not just any infant, Marina. I would want the infant to be my son. Rather, to be *seen* as my son."

She cringed at the thought of Easal taking over the body of a helpless child. How unsavory an idea, although she'd no doubt seen worse things. Odetta had been a cruel witch, after all. Having attended numerous ceremonies involving children, Marina wasn't surprised by much. The curse of no male children in O'Malley lands had required the blood of young males, she hadn't forgotten that. "Ye mean to keep yer power, even if ye must start over, from the beginning as a child."

"Aye, I do," he responded. "That is why the lass we choose as me wife must be suitable, to raise, essentially....*me*. If need be."

Moya tied the second set of leads around the large steed that stood regally next to the brown mare Darina had chosen. She knew that Patrick would be might angry with her for letting Darina ride, let alone bring along an elderly guest. But, she also knew the anger she was in for had she not done Darina's bidding. Lord Patrick O'Malley's wife was no stranger to her. No, Darina had quite nearly grown up in her stable, she had been always underfoot, and she was a little trouble-maker to say the least in her adolescence. She was as close a thing to having a child that Moya would ever know and she loved Darina dearly. It was her very ripe condition that troubled her. She knew very well Vynae would never approve of her riding so close to the babe coming, and that made her all the more hesitant.

"Are ye sure ye can handle the steed," Moya asked, directing her question physically to Airard but looking right at Darina. He smiled at her as he unsteadily took hold of the lead, and somehow managed to raise himself to mount. *Weak.* He looked incredibly weak to Moya and she wondered what would become of the pitiful two if one of them should suffer a fall or worse. Darina was in no condition to help him and he was definitely in no condition to help her. God forbid she should go into labor.

"How long do ye plan to be gone, milady?" Moya inquired.

"As long as it takes, Moya," Darina chastised, gruffly for affect. She glared at her with a disapproving, rebellious frown but broke into a smirk once she caught Moya's eye. Not exactly used to her station as Lord's wife, Darina had a bit of 'entitled Lord's daughter' still coming out. "I don't expect to be gone more than say, three hours," she offered. Stepping on the stool, Darina grunted and raised herself on the mare, landing with a thud. The mare jerked and resettled her footing.

"Where may I say ye are a goin'?"

"Ye can't," Darina rebutted. "If anaone should ask, we've gone for a walk, in the orchards. Darina grabbed the lead from Airard and set out of the paddock towards the open fields. The weather was good and the skies were clear, of that she was thankful. She just hoped the audience they sought was willing and would accommodate them. She didn't know how Airard knew about Covar, but the mention of his name was a confirmation of sorts. Perhaps now she would get the answers she sought about her son and their future. Her companion sought his audience for other, more pressing reasons she presumed.

fourteen

O'Malley Territory - The Island of Women

They had rowed for hours against the rough, choppy waters and the Island was finally within sight. Braedyn estimated another hour or two at most and they would set down on the shore. Finding the abandoned dinghy was a blessing, until they realized how far they had to go and how little strength remained among them. Orla's hands were bleeding and Naelyn did her best to tend to them.

"Let's jest rest here a bit, the wind is in our favor," said Naelyn.

"Aye," Braedyn replied. "I ken ye are right. We can rest here awhile," he said looking over at a sleeping Orla and back up at the clear sky. "She is might nearly worn out I suppose," he whispered.

"Ye care verra much for her, I can see that," said Naelyn. "What do ye suppose she feels for ye?"

Braeden grinned a devilish grin and settled the oars at the bottom of the dinghy before reaching for the skin of water. He took a long, slow swig before handing it to Naelyn. "I ken she likes me," he sighed, "she may even more than like me, it's hard to tell sometimes," he added, sighing for emphasis.

The clouds above them grew dark, an ominous sign Naelyn thought to herself. Rocking back and forth in the choppy water, she stabilized herself with both hands, one against each side of the dinghy. Unable to let loose of her fear of water, Naelyn continued the small talk with Braedyn. Anything to take her mind off the awful water and their predicament and what it was she was going to tell her sister, Gemma.

Gemma knew she had been cared for and practically raised by Odetta and she had overlooked much of her past. No doubt, Gemma probably feared her dead since she didn't arrive in O'Malley territory with the other Burke refugees. When Gemma found out she had been imprisoned by Easal and held against her will to do his bidding, would she believe her? Would the O'Malley clan accept her or send her back to Burke lands? And what of the dragon? Would they believe her story?

"Have ye plans for the future with her?" asked Naelyn, nodding in the direction of the sleeping Orla between them in the boat. "Have ye sights on marriage Braeden?"

"Aye," he replied, matter-of-factly. "She will be me bride."

"She will?"

"Aye, she will."

"And just what if she has something else to say about it," she asked concealing a grin.

"I'm sure she will, knowing Orla. But, I'm also confident she will come around to my way of thinking soon enough. She always does. Besides, it makes perfect sense we should be married. I will be Laird one day ye know, and she will be my Lady." His eyes twinkled at the thought. He had clearly put as much thought as his adolescent brain could muster into the idea of making a good match, for himself and his clan.

Orla moaned and shifted her weight against the floor of the small dinghy. Rubbing her eyes, she sank back down against the wet bottom in near surrender. They were all completely soaked, and worn out and bloody and beaten, but thank the gods the sun was out. At least they wouldn't "catch their deaths." Stretching her long arms overhead, Orla moaned one last, long moan before propping herself up on one arm to survey their predicament.

The island was in sight and a current seemed to be carrying them along. Neither Braeden nor Naelyn was rowing, but they were making headway in the right direction. She could be thankful she needn't row for the moment. Her hands had bled through the make-shift bandages, and Naelyn's skirt bottom was practically gone, but it had done the trick.

It would be a long, long time before she would ever trust Braeden O'Malley again. Of all the situations he had gotten them into, this was the worst. She would face terrible consequences when she got back, the least of which would be answering to Lord Patrick O'Malley. It was her mother she feared the most and her mother's sister, Odetta, that scared her even more. She voluntarily left the safety of the clan, and they must be fearing her dead at this point. How could she tell them what they found, and why they left? How could she explain that they conjured up their very own dragon?

Orla took a long, deep breath and sat up all the way, balancing herself by clutching tightly to the make-shift seat in front of her. Staring at the top of her bandaged hands, she realized it had suddenly become dark for a moment, then light again, and then dark again.

Either the sun was going behind the clouds or something was casting shadows on the trio as they rocked in the boat. She shuddered to think what would be large enough to leave that kind of shadow. Still drowsy from her exhaustion induced nap, she looked up to search Braeden's face.

"Braeden," she said softly.

"Aye," he replied, just as softly, never taking his eyes off the bottom of the dinghy.

"Do ye see that shadow?" she continued.

"Aye, I see it," Naelyn interjected from behind her.

"What do ye suppose...?" Orla began.

"Tis the dragon," Braeden responded calmly to the both of them. "It's been following us for several hours yet. Don't make any sudden moves now."

"If it's been following us Braeden, why on earth have we stopped rowing?" asked Orla, tears pooling in her eyes. "Why aren't we getting to the island as fast as we can?"

"Orla, if the dragon wanted us dead, don't ye suppose we'd be dead already? We can't outrun a flying dragon. Besides, there is nothing on that island that can save us from a dragon if it knows where we are."

"He's right," said Naelyn. "If this is the dragon you summoned, I don't think it means to kill you.

"Why do you suppose it's following us then?" asked Orla.

Braeden replied, "I guess we will find out soon enough."

fifteen

O'Malley Lands

Patrick and Lucian watched in astonishment from the battlements at the field below them. It was littered with soldiers, hundreds of thousands of soldiers, troops visible in every direction and their numbers stretched for miles upon rolling miles. It was an marvelous sight. They silently trained, in formation, in synchronicity and they were impressive. The sound of it was akin to what you might expect of the rush of angels wings.

"Phenomenal," whispered Lucian. "I am beyond words at this point," he muttered under his breath as he shook his head left and right. Turning to his immediate right, he greeted Kurt with a nod and motioned for Galen to join them as well on the west side overlooking the great plain adjacent to the shipyard.

"What astonishes ye more Lucian, that they are precise in their movements or that a blind mon leads them?" asked Patrick.

Lucian took a long deep breath and leaned his back against the stoney wall, crossing his arms for emphasis. "I suppose what astonishes me more than anathing is that ye took the advice of Odetta Burke. And - I can't say as I have as much faith in her as ye do."

"Ye called for me, Milord," Kurt interjected, bowing courteously before Lord O'Malley and nodding towards Lucian. "I've brought Galen as well, in case ye have need of spiritual counseling."

Lucian snickered and met eyes with Patrick. "He's no need of yer spiritual advice Kurt, ye know verra well we are druid priests, it's no' been a secret for some time now." Kurt nodded stoically and sent a cutting glance to Galen, the cleric who had taken his place as clan priest after he was stripped of his position.

"Thank ye Kurt, but that's no' why I sought ye," replied Patrick. "Galen, thank you for coming, but ye are dismissed," he said, adding to the mystery of the invitation. "Kurt, have some wine won't ye? And, take a seat, we've something of a delicate nature to discuss."

Kurt accepted the goblet offered by the servant and shot a wide gaze across the territory, noting with peculiarity the absence of Flynn, the Chieftain, in the fields. Instead, as noted by the flag-barer, there was Jamie Burke and his regiment and they seemed to be leading the current exercises. There were also the O'Malley soldiers, wearing the O'Malley tartan, and the Burke soldiers who were also wearing the traditional O'Malley tartan. Seeing as how the enemy was the remaining Burkes in Burke territory, there shouldn't have been any confusion between soldiers. There was also a tartan Kurt didn't quite recognize, it was similar to O'Malley plaid, but a different shade of blue.

"Pardon me, Milord," Kurt interrupted, "but what soldiers be they who wear the royal blue plaid?" he asked, leaning far over the edge to get a better view. "I've never seen such a pattern."

Lucian smiled and elbowed Patrick. "Yes, Milord," he said, "please do tell Kurt about those other soldiers."

"I canna' believe it!" Kurt added, clasping his hands above his head in disbelief, and then turning back around to take another look, stretching and leaning animatedly over the edge at this point.

"Patrick, they are..." Kurt began before taking another long swig of his wine. "They are..." he attempted again.

By now, Lucian was laughing out loud and Patrick was smiling a mischievous smile. They hadn't intended for this to be the manner in which Kurt was told, but it would have to do. "Kurt," said Lucian slowly, "the soldiers *are* indeed blindfolded."

"But, that's not the best part, ye know?" interjected Patrick, motioning once again for Kurt to take a seat.

"It's not?"

"Nay," broke in Lucian.

"Ye see the soldiers in the new tartan?" asked Patrick.

"Aye," whispered Kurt, turning back around in disbelief.

"Those soldiers are women."

It took some moments for the color to return to Kurt's face. Some long, intensely amusing moments for Lucian, who Patrick was either unable or unwilling to admonish. Before long, both men stood before Kurt laughing and jabbing with each other as they pointed at Kurt.

"Women?" Kurt repeated, disbelievingly, before turning back around to get a better look at the royal blood plaid. "Women?" he asked again, before finally sinking down into his seat in seeming defeat.

"Women," said Gemma, who was suddenly standing before the men. "And it's about time, don't ye think Kurt? she added smugly.

"Aye, Kurt, don't ye think?" added Ruarc, who was standing next to Gemma.

"Listen, ye may have gotten the wrong idea here," replied Kurt. "I only ever opposed the women fighting because of Rome, because of their requirements, it was no' me."

"It was no' ye?" snorted Gemma. "It was no' ye? Hogwash!"

"Never the mind," Patrick stated firmly. "We've no allegiance to Rome. We didna' call ye here to discuss the soldiers, well, not the fact that they are women anahow. I rather have no care as to anaone's opinion regarding that. The women have been protecting their island and this shore and our territory for longer than I've been here and they've every right to fight should they so choose."

"Aye," replied Gemma and Ruarc in unison. Lucian nodded in agreement and Kurt stared blankly in front of him.

"They *are* also blind-folded," whispered Kurt.

"Aye, they are," acknowledged Patrick, who stood at the precise moment Gemma and Ruarc took a seat. "And, there's an explanation for that as well. But - what we called ye here for is to discuss yer relationship with Odetta Burke."

"What?" gasped Gemma in disbelief.

"Aye," replied Patrick.

"Wait, shouldn't Flynn be here as well?" Gemma asked.

"Flynn has other, more pressing matters to attend," said Lucian. "He is making arrangements for military - uh - supplies," he blurted, seeking Patrick's approval with his eyes.

"Aye, he is," replied Patrick. "Critical military supplies."

"Weel' that settles it then," Missus Edwards hummed as she tugged at her skirts, attempting to lift her too large frame into what was left of the cart seat she was supposed to share with Aisling.

"Settles what?" Aisling retorted. "Settles what exactly?"

"Oh, never ye mind my dear one, I can see yer tired and there'll be plenty of time to work out the details."

"What details?," Aisling asked as she lurched forward and then backwards, holding on for dear life as the clackety cart made its way down the cobblestone path and outside of the gate surrounding Castle Burke. "What do ye mean? What details are ye referring to?

Don't ye think I shoulda' been part of the talks at least, seeing as how I may consider taking the Lord's hand an' all?"

"May consider?" the round-faced woman exclaimed. "May consider? I've got news for ye dear one. Ye've more than consider it, ye've accepted, and a mighty fine match I did get for ye if I do say so meself."

"Ye mean, ye've accepted terms without even consulting with me? I don't know how ye do things in Ireland, but from where I come, I have a significant amount of input and I intend to maintain control over me own...."

Missus Edwards grabbed Aisling about the shoulders before slapping her so hard she nearly fell out of the cart and onto the rocky terrain. Grabbing hold of her shoulders once more for affect, she pointed her bony index finger in her face and rambled something in a language that Aisling did not quite understand. "Now, just ye listen to me now," she whispered softly, but mouthed the words animatedly. "Ye don't ever want to let the Lord's guards hear ye say anathing at all like that. If it weren't for me child, ye'd most certainly be dead. As it stands, the other prisoners, uh, hmmm...I mean the others who survived the shipwreck have all been sold as slaves, at least by now."

Aisling gasped, but held tight to the burning hot tears that threatened to pour down her cheeks. She'd never been treated in such a manner in all her life. That Missus better learn her place and fast or she would find herself belly up in a shallow grave, a victim of the 'stomach bug.' "What do ye mean?" Aisling whispered back, taking note of the cart driver who appeared to be eavesdropping.

"Weel," Missus Edwards began again this time in a normal tone of voice. "...seems the Lord has takin' a like'n to ye and wishes to proceed with the marriage, *as soon as possible I might add*. I believe he said something about the day after tomorrow. At sunset no less. He wants a romantic setting, I presume. He was most impressed with his soon-to-be new bride," she elicited while wiggling her eyebrows.

Aisling cringed at the thought and rubbed the glass container in her cloak pocket. Would she have enough of the potion, or would she need to get away for a few hours to collect more supplies? Under no circumstances was she going to share a marriage bed with a man she had not even spoken a word to at this point. What a predicament this would be.

"But, but we didn't even speak to one another," replied Aisling. "He didn't sit next to me, he didn't speak to me, he barely even looked at me. He spent the entire evening at the other end of the table, consorting with that....that, that...old woman."

"That old woman," Missus Edwards began, "Could just be the key to yer salvation deary."

"What do ye mean?"

"Marina is Easal's, I mean, Lord Easal's most trusted advisor. She is the eldest council member remaining in Burke Lands since the exodus. Easal trusts her verra much. What Marina says goes. I'm sorry me dear, but ye shall be wed day after tomorrow, at sunset, on Sebastian Hill facing the shore. We've much planning to do and no time to waste."

sixteen

Finnegan Falls

Daenal rubbed her left arm again. It was paradoxically numb *and* painful and was throbbing such that it kept her from resting. She knew what was happening, she just wasn't ready to admit it to herself. She gathered from the muted cries from the back of the cave, that the small dragon struggled with sleep as much as she and that his mother had gone off hunting somewhere.

She was well fed, having finished off the last of the second hare and some kind of fish the elder dragon had brought before, but Daenal longed for fresh water. Cool, clear, refreshing water, it was tearing at her now. Dehydration. She feared that now more than she feared her captors. She was confused, dizzy, fatigued, unable to sleep yet unable to stay clearly awake. And - she had no way of communicating any of this with the dragons. Food was one thing, but water was quite another and Daenal knew it was only a matter of time. Only a day or two more and she would most likely fall asleep and never wake again. Never see her family, her precious Jamie, and never know what the meaning of all that had transpired really was.

Blue tussled a bit and sat right up on his wobbly legs, stretching his wings. Such as it was, his right wing extended and even bent some as it touched the cave walls, but his left wing, he kept protected and to his side. Unsure if he was malformed from birth, or simply protecting an injury, Daenal watched in astonishment at the majesty of the sight. His mother must be returning she thought to herself. It was uncanny how they sensed the other and Daenal drifted off in a haze of imaginations as to why human animals weren't the same.

Dizzy. I am dizzy again. She thought to herself or said out loud, she wasn't really certain which. Inching her way against the side wall of the cave, she took a seat when she sensed bottom. Blue was really restless now, bounding his way, haphazardly towards the mouth of the cave, towards the falling water and dimming sunlight.

Aye, she must be returning, she thought. *I must stand. But, I cannot. I am too weak, I am too dizzy, I have no strength. I can't seem to keep my eyes open. I must stay awake.* She awoke with a start. She was soaking wet and cold, drenched from head to toe. Rubbing her eyes, she peered out from between her fists in disbelief. She rubbed them once more, just to be sure, then removed her hands altogether.

"Why ye little varment," she yelled, the sound echoing throughout the cavern. Blue jumped back awkwardly, toppling over and to his left when he lost his balance. He did it again and what could have been buckets of water, sprayed against the wall behind her, drenching her in the process.

"Blue," she yelled again, laughing this time, "Are ye playing a game with me?" She stood up and moved two feet to her right where the pool of water was. He backed up a step and tilted his head slowly, examining her. First he titled left, then right, then he leaned in to get a better look at her. He stretched his long neck in her direction, tipping his head from side to side, as if inspecting her, sniffing all the while.

"I bet ye think I smell unusual, don't ye?" Daenal asked, reaching out a reluctant hand to touch the tip of his scaly nose. He remained patient throughout and even permitted her to stroke his check and down his neck before pulling away abruptly. She had gotten too close to his whithered wing and he was obviously sensitive or pained, she wasn't sure which.

"Come ye back and mayhap I can help ye," she called, but it was too late. He had already made his way back into the cave's recesses, for more sleep she presumed. Her own arm and shoulder blade became numb, limp and painful, all at the same time. A blinding headache shot up through the base of her spine and she clenched her teeth and eyes together, choking a strained groan. Daenal became dizzy and unable to stand on her own, so she leaned heavily against the back of the cave wall, hoping and praying for a merciful end to the painful episode that had caught her off guard.

What on earth did this all mean? Was she meant to help the dragon? Was this why she was here? She heard the snap and knew instinctively what was wrong. Her right shoulder was out of socket completely, leaving her arm limp underneath. But it wasn't really, was it? No! This must be what was wrong with Blue! For some reason, his right shoulder was out of the socket, all she needed to do was help him re-align it and reposition it into place and he would be fine. How on earth would she be able to help this young dragon, without getting herself killed in the process?

Daenal cried. She cried the first tears she had shed in some time since her mother had passed away, and she was so overcome with emotion, that she laughed simultaneously. So, this is what will break me? A crippled dragon? I can take anything —but a crippled dragon is the one thing in the world I will cry about? *What on earth is wrong with me?!* She half laughed, half screamed into the roaring water sound of the hollow cave.

Dervilla stood nervously in the doorway that led to Flynn's chamber, having stopped abruptly just before allowing herself to follow him inside. Against her better judgment, the most of her afternoon was spent, with him, and far too many mugs of her Aunt Atilde's bitter ale. The small trencher of roast guinea wasn't nearly sufficient to soak up the false courage which was slowly seeping from her. He was across the room now, having already shed his overcloak, lighting the lantern on his side table and straightening the bed linens. He motioned for her to join him at the round table near the fire, pouring her an already too large mug of elderberry wine.

She let out a relieved sigh before arduously stepping foot inside the doorway, in an animated fashion, as she was doing her best not to tip over. A loud hiccup escaped her throat and she raised her hand to her mouth in late protest. He grinned. Motioning for her to join him at the table, he pulled her chair out and waited patiently for her to complete her slow-motion tip toe.

"Dervilla," he whispered in her right ear as she sat, "I've no intention of taking advantage of ye."

"Oh, but I wish ye would," she said, out loud, before realizing she had.

"What did ye say?" he asked, in full chuckle now.

Her face turned the color of a ripe, red cherry and she threw her head on her hands on the table.

"Dervilla, how often do ye imbibe the spirits?"

"Not often," was her muffled reply.

Reaching across the table from his seated position, he grabbed her right hand and lightly stroked the inside of her wrist, sending shivers through her. She raised her head and locked gazes with him. Cognizant of the affect he was having, she attempted to remove her hand from his grasp, but he did not release it. Instead, her pulled her closer and lay a soft kiss on it and positioned his chair closer to hers.

"Flynn," she began, before remembering herself, "Chieftain Montgomery," she corrected, "forgive my impropriety, but I must get on, be about clan business. I shouldn't tarry, lest Lord O'Malley become sorely disappointed. My behavior is simply inexcusable. I am afraid I haven't acted much the lady today and for that I beg your forgiveness."

He smiled into her hand and whispered something she couldn't quite make out. It was the wet sensation his tongue left that shook her. She knew she would melt right there, where she sat, if he let out another warm breath against her palm. His tongue drew circles in the palm of her hand. He suckled her index finger and edged closer to her, closing the gab between their chairs as he placed his left boot on the ground between her right and left feet.

"Chieftain Montgomery," she sighed, "I really must be going. My presence here could send the wrong, uh, message to the others. I wouldn't wish to bring reproach upon my clan, my fellow soldiers or to ye, milord."

"Hush," was the soft reply in her right ear. "Let me worry about the others. I havena' finished me lunch and I intend to feast, Dervilla, on ye." His left hand rested slightly above her right knee and his tongue began a teasing kind of torture along her neck.

"Flynn," she gasped. "I am in no way prepared to...that is, I havena'...I mean, I wouldna' be inclined to..." the words escaped her, but she somehow knew that words would not be enough. Suddenly, she snapped to herself and shot straight up, out of her chair. She wasn't exactly sober, and most definitely not completely drunk. She managed to not sway but stood upright as she cleared her throat. She positioned herself between Flynn and the other side of the table and just stood there, motionless, for what seemed a millennia.

"Dervilla?" he asked, inquisitively.

"Milord," she responded, not sure what else to say.

"Have I frightened ye?"

"Nay, milord. I must be off, now," she said. Tears began to pool in her pale green eyes and she turned to look down, hands straight at her side as if reporting for duty. She clenched hard on her teeth and swallowed a heavy gulp in the back of her throat. It was too late. First one, then two, then another and soon her pale, freckled face was moist with the unwelcome tears. *I will no' break down,* she thought to herself.

What have I done? Dear God I've been too forward with Patrick's sister-in-law, and she is one of my soldiers. I will face disciplinary charge. And worst of all, I have offended someone I care about.

Flynn rose from his seat and stood to face Dervilla, raising his hands in mock surrender. Making sure not to get too close, he spoke softly. "Dervilla, if I have in any way offended thee, I beg yer pardon. I may have mistook our time together as a confirmation of sorts that mayhap ye felt the same of me as I do of thee?" he asked inquisitively.

She nodded, the tears having slowed a bit, and wiped the bigger portion of her wet face with the back of her tunic sleeve before resuming her position. "Aye," she ventured, sheepishly.

"I realize that in addition to being a member of Patrick's family, that I am also your superior with regards to this military."

She nodded again.

"I would hope that this occurrence wouldna' find ye distressed or perplexed to the point of seeking remedy or protection, from either the Lord or the clan council?" he asked, sheepishly, peering down to read her eyes.

She ventured her eyes upward to meet his gaze, providing a slight measure of reassurance to him, that she did not, in fact, seek to tarnish either of their reputations through petition. Their locked gaze forced another flow of tears that spilled over her already wet lashes, and her bottom lip quivered.

"Dervilla," he whimpered, motioning with his arms, "May I?"

She nodded again and met his embrace halfway, sobbing uncontrollably in his arms.

"Dervilla," he whispered, "I am so verra sorry, lass. What have I done? Won't ye please tell me?" Straightening somewhat, he felt her soft embrace turn rigid again. Unable or unwilling to permit her to form another wall between them, he held her tighter, closer to himself and whispered soft comforts in her ear. "Dervilla, what is it?" he asked again, his warm arms inviting her confession.

"I, I...I've neva'", she began, "and I'm no' sure if I'm rea...."

"Shhhh...." he replied, and pulled her closer. "Did ye think me a dishonorable mon, Dervilla?" She shook her head no. "Did ye believe I intended to take advantage of ye? Do ye think I planned to 'ave me way with ye and send ye off as if ye meant nothing to me?"

She sobbed again, loosening her grip about his waist.

He let her go this time, dropping his arms to his side, but grasping her hands with his own. He held up his kerchief as a peace offering and watched silently as she availed herself. When she had dried the last of her tears, he pulled her chin up to meet her eyes. "Dervilla, I am no' a devilish mon. My feelings for ye are sincere and *honorable*."

She looked down, but he refused to release her chin. "Look at me."

She raised her moist eyelids to meet his stare. "I'm sorry," she said.

"Ye don't need to be sorry, Dervilla."

"It's just that...well, I'm not good with...it's not my intention to..."

"Dervilla," he started, "are ye innocent?"

"Aye," she replied sheepishly.

"Are ye embarrassed because of it?" he prodded.

"Aye, I am."

He hugged her tightly and chuckled, sending shivers up her spine. "Dervilla," he laughed even more, "We are the same."

seventeen

O'Malley Territory

It had taken nearly an hour longer than Darina estimated to arrive at the top of the ridge. Not only was her size an imposition, but Airard's breathing had become labored and they stopped every so often for him to rest. The scented eucalyptus sachets provided by Vynae afforded him some brief relief, but Darina feared he was near to becoming untreatable. His palour was ghostly, his hands were feeble holding the reigns and the crackling sound emanating from his lungs told its own story.

He was adamant he would see Covar, and seeing how she had her own business to attend with the ethereal giant, Darina made no argument against their trip. She would have some answering to do, of that she was sure. There was no way she would make it back to the stables, or to the keep without her absence being noted. Patrick would thrash her with his tongue, but for now at least, he couldn't do it with his mind. She had long since locked him out of that private space, and with good reason.

"Ye wait here," whispered Airard against the wind. But, she knew what he said just the same, having read his puckered lips. He slid down the side of his horse and handed her the reigns. His face brightened a bit when just above them on the crest they heard a familiar whirling sound and saw a bright light encapsulating the ridge.

"Covar," she muttered. Airard nodded and smiled, clasped his hands behinds his back and disappeared into a fog of silver light. After she had managed to climb down from her own horse, Darina made a rough pallet on the grass and lay down for a quick nap. The smell of the outdoors and warm sunlight quickly sung her into a sleep-like trance.

She was tired; physically mostly but also mentally. The months following her marriage to Patrick had been filled with stress, turmoil, fear, threats of impending war, and family drama. Drama she knew wasn't likely to end anytime soon. Her energy was nearly completely gone and she longed for the care-free days of her youth. She longed for the days before the reality of her responsibilities as Lord's wife set in and threatened to drown her.

She could see him, in the distance, her handsome Highland warrior. He was calling and beckoning for her to join him. He was just ahead, above the ridge, near the falls, where they would swim and sunbathe and picnic under the stars. They hadn't taken a trip after their hurried nuptials, they hadn't taken any time for themselves at all. Instead, they were forced to jump in, right from the start, with the delicate affairs of protecting their clan, their village and not only their people, but the Burke's people as well. And, she had become pregnant, almost immediately.

Their days were fast and furious and filled with challenges and danger at every turn. Darina was still mother to her younger sisters, who had all been left orphaned. There was nothing of Darina left any longer. It seemed as if she owed her life and soul to others. *Always the others.* Nevermind the turmoil burning inside of her, the secret she couldn't share with anyone, not ever her Patrick. She feared what it all meant and hoped against hope that it wasn't an omen of things to come, or confirmation that she had completely lost her mind.

He was there, still, calling for her. His long hair was blowing in the breeze, and his chiseled, tanned features beckoned to her. Arms outstretched, he continued to summon her, but she was never quite able to reach him. Ever in the distance, he was growing further apart from her now, sliding backward in a vortex of fog and mist. His voice trailed off, and he no longer called to her. Had he given up? Had he found another? Hot tears moistened her cheeks and she lay quietly, silently searching for a slumber that never came. She mourned for her love, the life they could not have and the long-neglected passion she feared was gone forever.

"Darina."

She struggled to sleep or to wake, she wasn't sure.

"Darina."

She tossed and turned and felt the weight of the baby she carried shift to her right side, sending a cramp across her rib cage and down through her hip.

"Darina," it said again.

Startled, she sat up on the pallet and straightened her cloak. A warm, weathered hand stroked her forehead, clearing her hair from her eyes. "Darina," Airard repeated, "I am finished here.

"I must ha' dozed off," she replied, attempting to stand. Airard chuckled and motioned for her to move over instead, taking a spot next to her on the blanket.

"Is it my turn?" she asked.

"Nay," he waved her off. "Covar is gone now."

"But - I needed to see him."

"Aye, I know. He gave me a message for ye though, to take back."

"What do ye' mean? Are ye not coming back, Airard?"

Airard smiled and grabbed her right hand in his. "Me days are numbered lass. I will stay here, with Covar," he smiled. "T'wil be easier for evaone this way."

Tears crowded Darina's eyes and threatened to plunder her cheeks. What on earth would she tell Patrick? He would be so angry with her for leaving Airard here. He would blame her, and she would have no defense at all if he believed her that is.

I will deal with Patrick meself Darina.

She covered her mouth with her hand in astonishment. Airard, did ye read my thoughts?

Aye, I did. Up here, with Covar, there is no reason to disguise your thoughts me lass.

"I'm scared, Airard. There are things, things I do not even know how to talk about that, I just don't know to explain that....."

"Darina, ye've no reason to explain to me, and ye've no reason to fear either." Airard grabbed her around the neck and hugged her to himself. With shaky hands, he lightly stroked the back of her shoulders. "Ye are most definitely fulfilling a unique purpose, Darina. Ye and Patrick. There are so many things working in and around ye, and your clan, ye are blessed by the gods and it won't be long 'til ye see just that. Ye are surrounded with blessings, not curses, as ye believe."

Darina sobbed.

"Tell Patrick to follow the sun," he said.

"Follow the sun?" she asked, inquisitively.

"Patrick will know what that means, Darina. And - ye shall call him, Rory," he added, pointing to her swollen belly.

"What?"

Covar said that ye shall call him, Rory.

"My babe? It *is* a boy, I knew it," she smiled, imagining Vynae's soon to be astonishment.

"Aye."

"Rory, after me uncle?" she asked.

"Nay," said Airard, shaking his head and pointing to her belly, "Rory. After his, *great-great-great-great-great-great-great-*grandson.

eighteen

The Island

i must speak to you now," the voice rang in Gemma's mind. Or was it her ear? She wasn't sure, she just knew she was bone tired and she had just gotten the last of her little ones to finally bed down. Drums were calling from across the island and no doubt the festivities would begin soon, but this was no bacchanal in which she would participate. Her littlest was just beginning to walk and her eldest was just now big enough to help. Her maidservant had already left for the festival and Gemma was on her own for the evening. Between her and her four small daughters, there wasn't enough time in the day, or hours at night to catch up on sleep. No. She wouldn't entertain the voice, not at this hour. Her wine was taking affect, and she admonished her brain to take note of the matter and to just be quiet.

'But, I must speak to you. Now," it countered, rubbing her on the shoulder this time.

Gemma tossed a bit and rolled over, rubbed her eyes with both fists, and swung the coverlet off the bed and onto the floor. Positioning her feet over the side of the bed, she managed to prop herself up on shaky arms and stare straight into the eyes of seven-year-old Maeryn, who appeared just as startled as she to be awakened.

"Mammy," she began, "The bairns are all still asleep."

"Aye, good Maeryn. That's a good lass. What do ye need baby?" she asked.

"Nothing, mam."

Gemma looked around the cottage to see that in fact, the other three girls were all bundled up and bedded down behind the drape screen, and one was even snoring in cadence with the drums. "Maeryn, what do ye need lass?"

"Nothing, mam," Maeryn repeated, confused.

"The why did ye wake me, lass?" Gemma retorted, just as confused.

"I didn't mam. The lady outside did."

"What lady, Maeryn?" Gemma asked startled.

"I don't..I didn't see her. I heard her, mam. When I made to open the latch on the door, she bid me get ye instead. She wouldn't come inside. She told me to look after me seestas as she had need of ye this eve."

Gemma's heart froze. Was there someone here to take her babes? They weren't male. She couldn't imagine why anyone would want to kidnap her children, aside from the fact she was the Ruire, and they could hold them for ransom.

"I must speak to you, now. Her life depends on it."

Gemma's breath caught in her throat and she grabbed Maeryn about the shoulders. "Listen," she whispered. "Maeryn, I fear we may be in danger. Get ye that dagger I had made for you, and go stand with yer seestas. If ye hear me say it's time for tea, take the babes to the Missus O'Reilly's cottage, ye ken?"

Maeryn whimpered but did as she was told. Gemma dressed as quickly as she could and jumped into her boots, donning her overcloak and grabbing her sword simultaneously. Grabbing a lanthorn from her sideboard, she softly opened the latch on the cottage door, motioning for Maeryn to lock it behind her as soon as she was over the threshold.

"Good eve, Milady," a strong male voice greeted.

Relieved to see an O'Malley soldier down the cobblestone pathway, Gemma greeted back and pretended to shuffle the stack of firewood just outside her door.

"Anathing I can help ye with mam?" he asked.

"Nay, nay - I'm jest a little restless that's all. I think the drums are keeping me up. Thank the goddess me bairns could sleep through an earthquake though," she joked, hoping to throw him off her nervousness.

"Well, good then," he replied, "I'll be moving along. Good eve', milady," he said as he turned and walked the other direction.

Gemma stood for several moments and surveyed the area. It was dusk, the drums were growing louder and the light from the surrounding cottages was slowly diminishing. All that was left for many was the tell-tale sign of peat moss smoke burning through the tops of chimneys. Nothing seemed amiss. It would be nigh impossible for anyone who didn't belong on the island to be wondering about. The ferries had closed many hours before and the placement of the O'Malley sentries, over whom she had fought Patrick and lost, were at their posts, standing guard or patrolling.

"I must speak to ye. Please, do not be afraid."

"Where are ye?" asked Gemma, hands now trembling. "Show yourself."

"I am here, behind the barn. My appearance may frighten ye, and I don't want that. I don't."

"What's wrong with ye?" asked Gemma, walking slowly toward the stables. The horses were silent, but the goats were rustling, and they sounded upset. "Tell me, why would ye frighten me? Not much frightens me. And - why must ye see *me*?"

"I cannot communicate with her, I've tried," the voice said. "I need ye to come with me, so that we can tell her what she needs to do."

"Who, who are ye talking about?" Gemma asked, nearing the side of the barn.

"Please, stop," the voice said.

Gemma complied but grabbed tighter to her sword.

"I need to return her," the voice continued. "But I can't without her help first, and I can't seem to make her understand that."

"Who, who are ye talking about?" asked Gemma.

"Daenal."

Gemma's heart stopped in her chest and she froze in her tracks. "Ye have

Daenal?"

"Aye."

"Where do ye have her?"

"At the falls."

"Is she alone?"

"Nay, she is with my son."

"What does Daenal call ye?"

"She calls me Red."

"She is your niece, I don't understand why ye wouldn't want to do anathing about the fact that she is missing?" Odetta questioned, adding a small curtsey before standing bolt upright and leaning her left hand on the side Jamie Burke's table in the O'Malley great hall.

He continued his assault on the turkey leg in his right hand and wiped his left hand on the cloth in his lap. Her requests were becoming more and varied over the passed few weeks and nothing was so important that he need miss his evening meal. Jamie had even agreed to Patrick's request to hold off searching for his beloved Daenal, and now here she was again asking for yet another favor. His mother was becoming a big pain in his wide Irish arse.

"Sit, sit," he beckoned through chews. Motioning for a servant to bring her a trencher, he pulled out the empty chair beside him and she took residence. "What is it now? Ye say she's been missing? How long again?" he asked.

"More than a day, at least that's what I can gather."

"Her *mathair* doesn't know? he asked sarcastically.

"Nay, Raelyn has gone to McTierney lands with Cordal."

"And, exactly how many summers is this lass?" he queried while catching the eye of the wine bearer. "Here, have some wine," he said as he pushed a goblet in front of her plate.

"Twelve, wait, thirteen, maybe thirteen. I can't remember right now."

"I wouldna' worry if'n I was ye," he chuckled. "She is probably out with her friends getting into some good mischief, is all."

"I don't think ye understand, Jamie," Odetta whispered, watching the faces of those in the hall who were watching her. "We intend to make war with the Burkes at mid-day tomorrow during the eclipse."

"And - what of it?"

"And - if she is no' found before then, she may be trapped in the middle of something we canna' get her out of. That is if she isn't already a prisoner of Easal."

"Ye think he would have use of her as a prisoner? What, to hold her for ransom or some other such nonsense?"

"I think he has her already," Odetta replied, burying her head in her hands. How was she going to tell them what she knew without causing them to distrust her even more than they already did.

"I know because me spy brought me word that they do."

Jamie put down his food and turned to face her. Her aura was blue and he sensed she was telling the truth. "How....just how do ye know this?"

"Because, he brought me proof," she said, fumbling with something in her lap. "They have harmed her as well. And - I feel just awful about that," she began to weep.

"What did he bring ye? What is that?" Jamie asked, staring at her fumbling hands. "What is that, Odetta?"

"Jamie, it's is her finger."

"Her finger?" asked Flynn, who had happened upon the conversation. "What are ye talking about?" he grinned as he filled Jamie's mug with more ale before sitting down across from the two. Lady Burke, are ye alright? Ye look pale," he said, reaching a concerned hand her direction across the table.

"Nay, I'm not alright. I've just received the worst possible news. And - I am not sure what can be done about it," she added before storming out of the great hall in tears.

nineteen

Burke Land

She was light headed and the blood was everywhere. She could hear Missus Edward's muffled groanings and the sound of her rolling about in the corner of the cottage, *still tied up*, she presumed. Ochnar hadn't bothered to tie her up, he knew she would faint and remain unconscious for some time after what he had done, and that would give him time to get away.

It would take him an hour or more to get to Odetta. What he would bring her would most certainly usher in the war that his master Easal so clearly desired. A pinky finger and a ransom demand and they would be well on their way to getting the Nexus and sending Easal on his way. And then he, Ochnar Callahan, would be Lord of Burke Lands. He was the closest living relative of the late Burke Lord remaining in the territory and he would take up the mantle as clan leader.

One swift slice of his sharpened dagger and the tip of her left pinky finger was gone. She cursed, staggered and passed clean out, right there in the cottage. Missus Edwards made to come at him with her carving knife, but he knocked her down and tied her up. How could these silly women possibly understand the bigger picture?

Once Odetta got word that Easal held the lass and sought a ransom demand for her return, the O'Malley's would finally agree to meet in the Valley at high noon tomorrow. The war would be on, they would soon occupy the Island and the search for the Nexus would be in full swing. Easal promised to declare Ochnar Lord as soon as he had the Island as his own. Then he, Ochnar, would marry Aisling instead. Marina was clear this was the only way. And - they were to have an heir, right away, *as soon as possible* she said. Aisling would make him a fine bride, especially now that she knew who was going to be in charge. The little matter of a missing pinky finger would cause him no distress.

Odetta was shocked, outraged and clearly shaken up. She was not herself, clearly. Not even close. The sign of blood was nothing she would have flinched at before. What had become of the evil witch? Had she gotten soft?

Ochnar was as direct as he could have been. "We have the lass, and unless ye can get the O'Malley's to agree to meet us at noon on the morrow for the battle, I will return with her head." She nearly passed out.

"I understand," she repeated, unconsciously perhaps, over and over again. "I understand," she said, looking him the eyes. She carefully re-wrapped the package, stood, looked him the eye again and said, "Ye must be off. Tell Easal we will meet him on the morrow."

Ochnar tilted his head, searching her face for any sign of the Odetta he once knew. "Would ye like my report on Easal, milady?"

"Nay," she said nervously pulling at her skirt. "Ye must be off, and I have plans to make. Ye best be on yer way if ye intend to get off without being seen."

Patrick hadn't meant to doze off. His solar was unusually warm and the last few nights had proven difficult to sleep. It was the same dream, or day-dream or hallucination, he wasn't quite sure anymore. She was there on the ridge, backing away from a group of people, in some peril he presumed. Her falcon was circling overhead. She was dangerously close to falling over the cliff, but she continued to back away anyhow. He was calling to her, but she wasn't listening or she couldn't hear him. A man was raising an arrow in her direction and she was terrified at the sight.

He had been having the same dream about Darina since before they even met, and he still didn't now what it all meant. Except this time, his beloved was very clearly pregnant.

"Patrick." His thoughts were interrupted by Flynn.

"Aye," he replied.

"Patrick, we have need of ye in the council chambers," he said forlornly.

"Has something happened?" he asked hesitantly.

"Aye, it has. Something critical is requiring your attention. I've gathered the others, let's be on our way," Flynn said. Fanai sat obediently at Patrick's feet. The hound hadn't left his side since Darina left with Airard, and Moya wasn't any help at all when he questioned her. His wife was strong-willed and no doubt she would be back soon, he just wished she had taken her guard with her. She had gone through six of them in the last few weeks, and Patrick was at a loss as to what to do about it.

"We are here," Patrick said before stepping into the council chamber and noticing Odetta and Jamie Burke were also there. "What's going on?" he asked, clearly concerned.

"Patrick, Orla has been taken by Easal. He is holding her unless we agree to meet tomorrow at noon in the valley to do battle," said Jamie.

"And - how do we know this?" asked Patrick.

"His *mathair* has a spy," bellowed Ruarc, accusingly.

"A spy? asked Flynn. "Ye have a spy in Burke Lands?" the chieftain roared.

Odetta hung her head low and weeped. "Aye, I do. 'Tis Ochnar, a distant cousin on me mathair's side. I've had no reason not to trust him until today. He brought word of Orla's capture, and....this," she said, holding out the wrapped cloth containing the finger.

"What is that?" Lucian inquired.

"'Tis her finger, her left...p...pi...pinky finger," she muttered between tears.

"Let me 'ave a look a' it," Flynn demanded, gesturing for Odetta to hand it over.

"Tell me," he said, "how old is Orla?"

"She is nearly thirteen summers," Odetta replied. "She has been like me own daughter, I raised her meself, to keep her safe from Easal."

"This finger is too large for a thirteen-year old lass," said Flynn. "This belongs to someone else. They are toying with us."

"But, Orla is missing," Odetta said, "And so is Braeden."

"Braeden is missing?" yelled Patrick. "Why wasn't I told?"

"Hold on, hold on!" Ruarc replied. "Orla and Braeden are recovered. They were found two hours ago on the Island. They are a little worse for wear and have a story to tell mind ye, but they are fine, just the same. They are now recovering at the Inn, Minea is seeing to that."

"Then whose finger is that?" Patrick asked.

Flynn grew pale and sweat dripped from his brow. He sat down with a hard thud on the bench in front of him, still examining the contents of the cloth. "Patrick, this is Aisling's finger."

"Aisling?" Dervilla piped up from the doorway. "Aisling, your former betrothed?"

"Aye."

"How do ye know that is her finger?" Patrick asked.

"Because of the scar here, right on the tip," he pointed.

twenty

O'Malley Territory

his mouth tasted like the sweet wine they shared with their supper. His right hand was gently rocking the sleeping babes in the bassinet beside their soft feather bed while his left hand was inching its way up, under her shift. She leaned into his embrace and stroked the back of his neck with both hands.

"Parkin," she whispered into the darkness. "Are the bairns asleep?" asked Kyra.

The movement of his right hand confirmed they were, and she was soon swept up, into his arms and carried gently to the sheep skin rug which lay before the fireplace. He spread her hair out, around her face and marveled at its length. She stopped cutting it when she grew round with her pregnancy. She couldn't ride after all, and had no need to fit it into her helmet. It was nearly passed her shoulder blades and beautifully wavy. Her face was aglow with the light set off by the small fire and her lips were parted, ready for his advance.

He leaned in and tongue met tongue, in a tender dance. So gentle were his movements, she barely felt her shift being ripped from the bottom to top. His warmth was unmistakable, however, and she arched her back in response and surrender.

"Kyra," he moaned into her mouth before trailing kisses all along her jaw line and then from the neck to shoulder and back. "I can't get enough of ye." His mouth found her breasts and gently caressed the swollen mounds, careful not to use too much pressure. "How much longer will ye feed the babes?" he asked chuckling at the moisture which sprayed suddenly across his cheeks.

"Just a few more moons," she giggled, grabbing his head with her left hand forcefully, in mock attack. He reciprocated in kind and brought her up to meet him, supporting her weight with his right arm. He locked eyes with her and drank in her beauty, so unashamedly open was his worship and he kissed her again, forcefully this time.

"Parkin, I'm not sure it will matter though," she gasped, in between his assaults.

"Ye are mine, Kyra."

"Aye, ye own me Parkin, body, and soul. Well, at least soul, anaway."

He stopped his attack on her neck and looked up. "I own ye, *body* and soul, Kyra." He followed that with a playful smack on her bum and redirected his intentions to her luscious hips.

"The twins, they may have something to say about that," she mused as the evidence of their hold on her dripped down her belly.

"I plan to stake my claim soon enough," he quipped, as he lay her back down on the rug and hovered over her, leaning up on one arm while the other found its rightful place under her head. His heat grew rigid against her hip and his left leg swept up over her and down again on the other side.

"Parkin," she whispered softly.

"Aye, me love," he replied, deep in concentration.

"I've something to tell ye, and I hope ye'll be happy about it," she said.

"Can it wait, love?" he asked, inching his member close to her slick, throbbing entry.

"I fear ye'll be wanting to know, first...before...well. Ye'll want to know love," she said grabbing hold of his throbbing cock and stroking it lightly. His face wore a mask of ecstasy or anguish, she wasn't sure. He lay a gentle kiss upon her forehead and bid her continue.

"Parkin, ye won't own me body just yet, I'm afraid."

"I'll own it anatime I intend," he said playfully, moving his swollen tip inside her just a bit. She arched reflexively sending him deeper than she intended. He grinned a devilish grin and stabilized his arms underneath, never taking his eyes off hers.

"Tell me why ye say such, Kyra?" he asked, licking his lips and instinctively grinding his hip against hers, eliciting a delicious moan from his bride.

"Because, Parkin, I am with child, again."

He stopped, frozen it seemed, and closed his eyes tightly. A tear rolled from the corner of his left eye and landed on Kyra's cheek. "Parkin, have I upset ye?"

He shook his head no but released his position to lay next to her on the rug on his back. Grabbing her by the shoulders, he pulled her onto himself to rest her head on his chest and he weeped. She stroked his arm with her fingertips and asked again, "Parkin, have I angered ye?"

"Nay, Kyra. I am so verra happy."

"Then why are ye crying, my love? My body is yours, body and soul, ye know this Parkin. I was only toying with ye."

"I know Kyra," he whispered.

"What is the matter then?" she asked.

He was silent for what seemed a long moment, and then asked, "Kyra, how far along are ye?"

"Nigh to seven weeks," she said, adding, "At least according to Vynae.

"And the babe, it's alright?" he asked.

"Aye, Vynae assures me all is as it should be."

He whimpered and pulled her close to himself, kissing her forehead, but no longer hiding his tears.

"Parkin, what is wrong?"

"Kyra, I am just happy. Just verra, verra happy. I feared with the trouble ye had birthing the twins, that ye may wish or may not even be able to have more children. I wanted a child of my own - with ye Kyra, one that was ours. Ye know I love the babes, they are mine just as if I'd sired them meself. But - a babe of my own. I never dreamed we could have a babe of our own. I am so very happy, Kyra. So, verra, verra happy."

They flew over the village and along the shoreline for some time. Higher and higher they flew until the lights from the festival were all but specks of dust behind them. Even the sound of the drums had lessened and was instead replaced by the whirling of clouds beside and behind them. Gemma mustered all the courage she had in order to shape-shift in front of Red, but she had done so. Daenal's life depended on her ability to translate the communications of Red to Daenal and Daenals' ability to trust Gemma in this very precarious situation.

Red was simply the most magnificent creature Gemma had ever encountered, in her life or in her dreams, either one. *Magnificent.* Yes, that was the only word one could use to describe the delicate monstrosity parting the clouds before her. Her wingspan alone had to be over twenty feet. They were getting closer to the Falls and Red appeared to being slowing and dropping altitude, so Gemma followed suit.

It's not far now. I will go in before you, then please, come in behind me, Red spoke to Gemma's mind.

Am I losing my mind? Gemma thought to herself.

No, you aren't, came Red's gentle reply.

As they grew closer to the Falls, they heard the anguished cry of Blue. The screeching bellows subsided, then re-started again, and the cave's echo propelled the noise out through the falls, and into the atmosphere with force. Something was killing the young dragon and Gemma was scared to know the truth. Surely, Daenal couldn't be hurting the dragon?

She is not hurting him. She is finally doing what I brought her here for in the first place.

What do you mean? Asked Gemma with her mind.

She is a healer, I brought her here to help my fireling. She has finally realized that and he has finally as well it appears, said Red.

But why are ye....here? asked Gemma. *Where did ye come from, how long will ye stay?*

We were summoned, myself, my King, and our fireling.

Summoned, who summoned ye?

Covar.

τwenτy–one

O'Malley Castle
Council's Chamber

It wasn't like Lord Patrick O'Malley to lose his temper, let alone display it for the entire room to see. His voice was deeper, stronger and louder than anyone could have anticipated and when he roared the entire room shook. It was like the sound of a thousand lions and the echo itself was painful to the ears. His face was a deep red, then a stony gray and it looked as if his eyes would burst from their sockets. Slamming his right hand roughly against the council table, he rose, paced the room, roared again and slammed his right shoulder into the wall. The sentries guarding the door entered the room, astonished at what they saw. They were quickly dismissed by Ruarc and returned to their posts.

"Has he gone mad?" asked Dervilla, clearly concerned.

Flynn rose as well and paced in synchronicity with Patrick, back and forth and back and forth. Patrick roared some more, slammed his hand down against the table again and grew as pale as his under cloak.

"Leave him be," muttered Odetta. "He is fine. Leave him be."

"What?" yelled Ruarc. "What on earth has gotten into him? He is not a mon of temper and he's had no spirits."

"Odetta is right," said Lucian.

"How would that *witch* know?" asked Galen. "Has she cast a spell on him?"

Patrick bellowed louder this time before doubling over as if in pain, and then finally laying down on the hard, cold floor of the chamber, flat on his back. Dervilla made to attend to him, but Lucian stopped her before she could get within three feet.

"Leave him be for the time, he is fine," said Odetta again. "But, do go fetch Vynae, we will need her services. Tell her to bring turmeric and frankincense."

Patrick roared again and rolled around on the hard floor for what seemed a millennium. Unable to verbally communicate, his face went from ghastly white to blood red, over and over again. Finally, his movements softened and his roaring stopped.

"Ye think he's passed out?" asked Dervilla, clearly upset by the entire episode.

"I don't rightly know," replied Flynn, rubbing his chin and shaking his head.

They all turned around to seek counsel from Lucian, who was grinning from ear to ear. "Bring some ale, he'll want some of that I can tell ye. And stoke the fire, its a bit chilled in here."

"Lucian, what is going on, what is wrong with Patrick?" asked Dervilla.

"There is nothing in the world wrong with Patrick," interjected Odetta. "Can't ye see it?"

"See what?" asked Ruarc harshly. "He's behaving like a crazed animal. Rolling around and screaming and not telling us what he's so upset about. It's unseemly. He's throwing some kind of a tantrum and I'm not impressed, I'm not."

"See it?" asked Odetta, pointing to a now-sitting Lord O'Malley.

Leaning against the council chamber wall, Patrick sat rubbing his right arm and shoulder. He was also smiling.

"What on earth is going on here?" screamed Dervilla. "I've had enough of the theatrics, someone better blewdy tell me the truth, and right now, or so help me g...."

"Wait," interjected Flynn. "Patrick, your arm."

Patrick smiled and leaned awkwardly against the wall, propping himself against his arm.

"Patrick it's wonderful," said Lucian who hurried to help him up.

"What's wonderful?" asked Dervilla.

"Dervilla," said Patrick, "do ye see me right arm? 'Tis not whithered anamore. 'Tis strong and straight."

"Patrick, ye are healed," said Galen, in astonishment. "I canna' believe it. Your arm, 'tis whole. I canna' believe it."

"Why can't ye believe it?" asked Odetta. "Doesna' your God perform miracles?"

"Aye, I've just never seen one," replied the preist.

Darina purposefully ignored the pain in her right side, she didn't have time to think about what that might mean, she had to get home, back to the keep - and fast. Leaving Airard with Covar was harder than she anticipated. She knew she would never see him again, but was somehow comforted by the thought he was with Covar now. He needn't fear what was to come, and for some reason she understood that he would never really ever be truly gone.

She had grown fond of him and yearned for some company for her long ride home. Pulling his steed alongside her own horse, she carefully made her way down the side of the mountain, careful to watch their path. The sun was hanging low over the port in the distance, and it would be dark soon. She would have much explaining to do to Patrick, and she wasn't quite yet ready to open her mind to him again. There was so much racing in the background, dreams, and visions she couldn't explain, he would think her daft and she had no way to defend herself.

She looked up just in time to watch a shooting star pass over the Island. A good omen she prayed as she felt the heavy kick of her son. *Rory*. She repeated it out loud to herself. "Rory, my red king," she smiled and patted her belly. Patrick would be thrilled to hear they were having a boy.

Patrick, my beloved. I have to find a way to back to you somehow.

twenty-two

O'Malley Council Chambers

Dervilla sat motionless on the side bench behind the council chamber. In one day, she had loved and lost and she was emotionally spent. Any promise of a future with Flynn Montgomery was gone. It was clear he still cared for Aisling McTavish, as evidence by the look on his face when he realized she was the captive in Burke Lands. No doubt they would go to war with the Burkes, just as Easal had wanted, a condition of her ransom. They were all prepared for war. More than prepared, really, as it had been many years coming. The realization that the urgency set in for Flynn when his betrothed was mentioned was what sealed her decision.

There would be no future for her here. She would seek dissolution of her military commission and perhaps leave O'Malley territory altogether. There would be no suitable men for her. She wouldn't put her life in the hands of the annual clan games, and she couldn't possibly stay with Flynn here and married to Aisling, or worse yet, pining for a deceased love, a victim of the trappings of war.

No, she couldn't compete with that and she wouldn't.

"Are we all clear then on the timing of the attack?" asked Flynn, who was hovering over the drawings strewn about on the table.

"Aye. Aye. Aye," came the many and varied responses from the commanders who stood stoically in the back of the chamber.

"And, Dervilla," said Flynn, "have we secured the nets? And have we them all?"

"We do," she replied, matter-of-factly."

"And what shall be done if or when they deliver this Aisling person prior to flag-down"? asked Ruarc.

"They won't," said Odetta softly.

"How do ye know?" asked Dervilla.

"Aye, how do ye know?" asked Flynn. "Have ye held something from us?"

"Nay, nay, nothing like that," replied Odetta. "I simply misunderstood. Ochnar said 'the lass" and I assumed he meant Orla this entire time. Ochnar used Aisling to persuade us to war. Easal has every intention of marrying her tomorrow eve at sunset, after his victory, on the Island of Women. If I understand correctly the missive I received from Marina."

"Of marrying her? Easal intends to take Aisling as his bride?" asked Flynn.

"Aye, Marina made the arrangement and Aisling accepted willingly. I suspect Ochnar will be in a heap load of trouble when Easal realizes he took her finger."

Tears pooled in Dervilla's eyes and threatened to spill. Her head spun and she feared she may faint. No, there was a worst case scenario, her love's former betrothed could marry her clan's worst enemy and cost them all. Flynn's conflict over this new development would test the fortitude of any clan chieftain. How would he get on? How would she? He would be unable to hide his wrath, jealousy or need for revenge. She couldn't stand it and she wouldn't. She must leave, and now.

"I have a request, please," she interrupted the meeting. "I have a request, please, may I be heard?"

"Aye," replied Lord O'Malley. "What's your request Dervilla?"

Flynn looked up in astonishment and glanced at her sideways in question.

She ignored his attempts to get her attention and continued on. "I wish to petition for dissolution of my military commission."

"Why on earth?" asked Flynn. Suddenly afraid she intended to report him for inappropriate conduct, Flynn went to sit next to her.

"Effective when Dervilla?" asked Patrick. "We are to meet the Burke's in battle tomorrow at high noon in the valley. Do ye wish to leave a'fore then? Are you frightened? Has something happened? Is something wrong?"

"Nay, I am not frightened. As soon as the final outcome of the battle tomorrow is determined, and if it pleases milord, I would like to dissolve my commission then."

"I would have your reason," repeated Patrick. "Can ye give me a good reason?" he pressed.

"I...I don't know....what to say," Dervilla whimpered between tears. All eyes in the chamber were now on her, all the commanders included and she suddenly felt completely out of sorts.

"I can give you a reason," spoke Flynn, who rose and stood behind Dervilla, placing both hands on her shoulders.

"Ye can?" asked Dervilla, perplexed.

"Aye. I'd every intention of asking ye Patrick for Dervilla's hand prior to this moment, but I'll do it now.

Dervilla looked up in astonishment. "Flynn?"

"I am making my intentions known, and asking ye, Dervilla," he said, kneeling down next to her. Placing a tender kiss atop her right hand, he said, "Dervilla, will ye do me the honor of becoming me bride?"

Dervilla wept and stood, kissing him in acceptance of his proposal. The chamber erupted in noise, congratulatory cheering, and clapping.

"I'll wish to wed her this eve, tonight, prior to battle tomorrow. If it pleases milord?" Flynn directed to Patrick, who sought approval from Dervilla.

"Tonight it is then!" clapped Lucian, "'Tis a beautiful night for a wedding."

"Would ye have room for one more couple?" echoed a soft female voice.

Jamie Burke rose to his feet. He heard the voice, but he didn't believe it. The room was overcrowded with soldiers and council members and servants scurrying about, but he felt her presence nonetheless. A reverent hush came over the crowd as Jamie made his way around the room, searching for the voice.

"I am here," it said, from somewhere on his left. He turned, and maneuvered his way toward the sound. "Just in front of ye now."

Her aura was unmistakable, and his heart leaped in his chest.

"Would ye be wanting to marry this eve, my Jamie?" Daenal O'Malley asked the giant of a man who had won her heart as well as her hand.

"Aye. Indeed, I will," he said. "Indeed I will."

ABOUT THE AUTHOR

 Of Irish and English descent, Romance Author Delaney Rhodes is a native Texan from birth. She is a Graduate with double Majors from The University of Houston, in Law and Writing. She has two teenage daughters, and is married to an entrepreneurial husband. Three of her favorite people are her three rescued Russian Blue cats; Sebastian, Sasha, and Sissy. The family would not be complete without "13", an adopted Bearded Dragon.

Together they live life at a fast pace, enjoying each other and striving to help the world become a better place. Besides her writing and family, Ms. Rhodes is active in many charitable organizations that benefit animals and children, both through volunteering and fundraising.

Ms. Rhodes' writing was prompted and inspired by many hours of research and study into her Irish and Celtic family lineage and heritage. Many of the stories you will find in the chapters of her writings were birthed while striving to connect with those that had walked these paths and lived before her.

Delaney@DelaneyRhodes.com
http://www.DelaneyRhodes.com
http://www.facebook.com/delaneyrhodes
http://www.twitter.com/delaney_rhodes

More Titles By Delaney Rhodes

Celtic Steel Series

Book 1: Celtic Storms, February 2012

Book 2: Celtic Shores, May 2012

Book 3: Celtic Skies, August 2012

Book 4: Celtic Stars, March 2015

Book 5: Celtic Sun, June 2015

Skyelanders Series—*Coming Soon!*

Book 1, Skyelanders, Sacrifice

Book 2, Skyelanders, Sanctuary

Book 3, Skyelanders, Salvation